THE FISHMONGER'S DAUGHTER

Victorian Romance

FAYE GODWIN

Tica House
Publishing

Copyright © 2021 by Faye Godwin

All rights reserved.

No part of this book may be reproduced in any form or by any electronic or mechanical means, including information storage and retrieval systems, without written permission from the author, except for the use of brief quotations in a book review.

PERSONAL WORD FROM THE AUTHOR

DEAREST READERS,

I'm so delighted that you have chosen one of my books to read. I am proud to be a part of the team of writers at Tica House Publishing. Our goal is to inspire, entertain, and give you many hours of reading pleasure. Your kind words and loving readership are deeply appreciated.

I would like to personally invite you to sign up for updates and to become part of our **Exclusive Reader Club**—it's completely Free to Join! I'd love to welcome you!

Much love,

Faye Godwin

FAYE GODWIN

CLICK HERE to Join our Reader's Club and to Receive Tica House Updates!

https://victorian.subscribemenow.com/

CONTENTS

Personal Word From The Author	1
PART I	
Chapter 1	7
Chapter 2	15
Chapter 3	26
Chapter 4	35
PART II	
Chapter 5	45
Chapter 6	55
Chapter 7	63
Chapter 8	74
Chapter 9	84
PART III	
Chapter 10	95
Chapter 11	103
Chapter 12	109
Chapter 13	117
Chapter 14	128
Chapter 15	139
PART IV	
Chapter 16	149
Chapter 17	156
Chapter 18	162
Chapter 19	173
Continue Reading...	176
Thanks For Reading	178

More Faye Godwin Victorian Romances! 179
About the Author 181

PART I

CHAPTER 1

ABBIE HUGHES KEPT a wary eye on the brass-buttoned bobby on the street corner. It seemed as though he hadn't seen them yet; he was busy grasping the collar of a grubby, out-at-the elbows character who had pinched some of the half-wilted peaches right out of the grocer's window. Abbie could imagine how hungry the man must have been to steal from the grocer. She knew that hunger well – it gnawed at her own belly right now. She knew that desperation, and she had felt dismay when the grocer had shouted, "Stop! Thief!" and the clanging bell of the bobby had sounded around the corner.

One thing that was for sure—the policeman was deeply occupied in bellowing at the man, and he wasn't paying any attention to Abbie.

"We should go," hissed her little sister at her elbow. "While he's busy – before he sees us."

Abbie wasn't sure what it was about their tiny, grubby stand that made them such a target. If it wasn't the police chasing them off for being a public menace (presumably it was very menacing to sell thin bone broth to gaunt, grubby people), it was the nearby shopkeepers who didn't like their dirty faces and unwashed clothes detracting from the appearance of the street. But she knew she and Gail could get the stand packed up in a matter of seconds if they had to.

"Come on, Abbie," said Gail. Gail's eyes were wide and round in her pinched, dirty face, making her look older than her twelve years.

Abbie looked back at the line of people waiting silently for soup. Several of them had melted away at the appearance of the policeman, but a few remained, hopefully clutching their bowls and pennies. The pennies gleamed a little in the fading evening light. Abbie was acutely aware of how much her family needed them.

"Quick," she hissed, gesturing at the next customer.

The old man shuffled over to her, dropped a few pennies in her hand and passed her the bowl. Gail stared at Abbie, the ladle clutched in her hand. It had a broken handle. "Are you sure?"

"Hurry, Gail," said Abbie.

Gail shrugged and started spooning the watery mixture into the bowl. It wasn't much; a pale, oily substance, made from whatever tiny scraps of meat were left on the bones Abbie bought from the butcher, and maybe one or two wilted turnips if she could get them. But it was piping hot thanks to the wood fire crackling under the great old iron pot. The old man's eyes widened in glee as he wrapped his hands, encased in fingerless gloves, around the bowl.

"Next," hissed Abbie, shooting a glance at the policeman. He was binding the wrists of the thief, the grocer looking on with great contentment.

A few more people came up to the stand, and when the last scoop of broth had been scraped out of the pot, the policeman had just stuffed the thief into a frightening, barred wagon. Their time was up, and Abbie felt fear grip her as the grocer glanced around. All it would take would be for him to tell the policeman they had stolen something, and they'd be collared next.

"Time to go," she hissed to Gail.

The girls leapt into action. Gail doused the fire; Abbie pulled down the makeshift roof over their stall, made of sticks and rags, and rolled them into a ball. Gail grabbed the box they used as a table, Abbie seized the pot by one handle, and in a few minutes, they were jogging off down the street.

"Whew," Gail breathed. "That was a close one. I didn't like the way that bobby was looking at us. They don't care for us poor folk."

"Maybe some of them do, but I don't trust that grocer," said Abbie. She sighed. "We'll have to move again. We can't go back to that street now."

"It's a pity," said Gail. "We had enough business there."

"That's true. But we'll find business somewhere else," said Abbie. "Maybe the next street will have more people in it that buy posies. At least, they smell better than the bone broth."

"I guess," said Gail. "But I do like warming myself by the broth's fire."

"It's nearly summer." Abbie smiled. "Things are always better in the summer."

"And maybe, this summer, Patrick will come home," said Gail.

Gail had been saying it every summer for three years now, but Patrick never had come home. Sometimes he would send letters to his sisters, telling them about exotic countries and wild adventures on the seven seas. The letters made Papa proud and sad at the same time, and he would read them over and over again to the girls, squinting as he struggled to make out the words. Patrick had learned to read during better times – long before Abbie or Gail were born. Mama had still been alive and a housekeeper at a great manor house; Papa had still been a sailor, and even a first mate at one time.

Then Mama had died having Gail, and Papa had broken his leg in a storm. He never sailed again. He only lived in Patrick's letters, and then gazed misty-eyed at nothing when he had finished reading them, as if he could see once more the storm-tossed horizon that had always called his name.

As Gail and Abbie walked, the paving stones turned to mud underneath their feet, half-frozen as the winter still fought against relinquishing its hold on London. The smells of the dockside streets – fish and tar and salt and sea – began to fade, replaced by a more insidious stench—holding the sweet edge of death in its sickly odor. Around them, fewer and fewer buildings were built out of wood or stone. They began to give way to perilous little tenement buildings that fell in crooked heaps beside the twisted street like bent old beggars.

It was toward one of these tenement buildings that Abbie and Gail directed their weary steps. Dusk was coming quickly, speeding toward the Thames from the west, and the first street lamps were just being lit when they reached the rickety front door that had a plank missing near the bottom. A draft blew through it with a long, melancholy sound as Abbie pulled it open.

Their tenement was on the ground floor. Abbie was grateful they didn't have to carry their stand up the wobbling stairs. Her arms were already aching, her shoulders stinging from the effort of keeping a grip on the pot without letting its hot sides burn her. Gail nudged open a door to their left, and they stepped into the little room they called home.

It was a long, low room, perpetually smoky thanks to the chimney that hadn't been swept in decades. The black tendrils of smoke swirled and writhed in a nightmarish motion thanks to the draft that always blew in under the door and out through the many little gaps in the opposite wall, despite the rags and bits of old newspaper that had been stuffed into them, now blackened by soot. There were no windows, but the fire provided a flickering light, countered at the far end by a stub of candle burning valiantly in the choked air.

"Papa's home," gasped Gail, delight in her voice.

"He is indeed." Papa sat up, a tall, weary figure sitting on the little sleeping pallet in the back corner of the room. He unfolded his long arms, a chuckle splitting his grizzled beard. "Ah, my dear girls. Come here."

Abbie felt a rush of childlike glee as she put down the pot and hurried into Papa's arms. He enfolded both her and Gail with a crushing embrace. Despite the fact that he smelled strongly of the fish he hawked for the company that once employed him at sea, Abbie buried her face in his jacket. He still smoked a sailor's tobacco that smelled harsh and acrid and deeply homely.

"How was your day, girls?" asked Papa, leaning back and studying them. His eyes were the colour of a sea, and just as ever-changing; right now, they were a mellow blue, like a calm ocean lying flat beneath a sunny sky.

"It was all right," said Abbie. "We sold quite a lot of broth. I'll be able to buy us a week's coal tomorrow, if the rent's been paid."

"It has," Papa assured her. "Don't you worry, darling." He kissed her forehead; his beard was scratchy and his movements clumsy, but his eyes shone with sincerity. "And I've brought us some bread and coffee for supper."

"Mmm," sighed Gail. "Coffee."

"No sugar or milk this time," said Papa unnecessarily. He always said it; they never expected such extravagant luxuries, except on their birthdays, but Papa always seemed to feel guilty about it.

"I'll hang the kettle," said Abbie. "Gail, won't you wash out the pot?"

"Let me help," said Papa, standing up and moving toward the bucket of water.

"It's all right, thanks," said Abbie. "I think you should rest your leg." She kissed his cheek. "Rest now, Papa. We'll have supper in a moment."

Papa grumbled a little but limped back to the pallet and sank down slowly, wincing as his bad leg struggled to support his weight. As always, Abbie had to work hard not to think too much of Patrick. It had been weeks since the last letter from her brother. Part of her was always afraid that she'd lost him forever.

She scooped some water from the bucket in the corner into their kettle, careful only to fill it halfway; there was a hole near the top that would hiss and steam awfully if she made it too full. She hung the kettle over the struggling fire and opened the wooden trunk that served as their only storage space to retrieve three bent tin mugs.

Gail had put away the pot and was breaking the bread into thirds; judging by the crumbs, it was only slightly stale. Abbie made the coffee quickly, and they all three sat down around the trunk – which doubled as a table – and joined hands for Papa's habitual brief, gruff grace.

As soon as he said "Amen", Abbie was tearing into her portion of the bread. As watery as the bone broth was, the smell of it had been making her hungry all day long.

"I'm glad your street corner is treating you girls well," Papa said, eyeing the now-empty coal-scuttle in the corner of the tenement.

Abbie sighed. She had hoped to be able to wait until the next morning, or at least until Papa had a full belly, before breaking the bad news. "I'm afraid we won't be able to go back there, Papa," she said.

"Why not?" Papa looked instantly worried. "Are you all right? Did something happen?"

"No, but it nearly did," said Abbie. "A man stole from the grocer, and he called the police. The grocer is starting to get more and more annoyed with our stand being so close to his shop. He grumps at us all the time. I think he would have had the policeman chase us if we hadn't moved away as quickly as we did."

Papa sighed, looking tired. The expression lasted only a moment before he replaced it with his usual fond smile and laid a hand on Abbie's shoulder.

"Don't worry, darling," he said. "All that matters if that you and your sister are safe. I know you sold a lot of broth on that corner, but I'd actually be glad if you moved to another spot."

"Why?" asked Gail. "We made more money than usual there."

"It's too far from home." Papa shuddered, fear shining in his eyes. "You are only just making it home before dark. The wharves are a very dangerous place, my girls. You never want to be caught out there when it's dark. So many things…"

"… can happen to us. We know, Papa." Abbie smiled. "You and Patrick have been saying this to us for years. Don't worry. We'll be careful." She reached over and took his hard, knobby hand. "I know we have to be safe."

Papa nodded, relaxing a little. Abbie shifted a little closer to him.

"You don't have to worry so much, Papa," said Gail kindly.

"Oh, my dear girls, you know I do," said Papa. "You're all I have, except for dear absent Patrick." He wrapped an arm around Abbie's shoulders. "But you're all I need."

CHAPTER 2

ABBIE HUMMED to herself as she stirred the broth in the pot hanging over the fire. It was an absurdly big pot for the amount of broth she was making, but Abbie didn't care; she was mostly focused on how good their supper looked bubbling around in the bottom.

She and Gail had been gathering posies in a little park near the wharves when they had spotted a man hawking a few solid sides of beef – at a tenth of their usual price. When the girls had drawn nearer, it had become evident that there was a reason why the price was so low. The beef smelled strong. But the smell was not yet sour, and they'd had a successful morning selling posies. Abbie had been quick to splurge on one of the beef cuts. She had to hustle home quickly with it, though, or it would soon be too bad to eat.

Now, it had lost its acrid scent, and the promising lumps of meat boiled merrily along with a couple of potatoes that Abbie had been able to scrounge. She'd even gotten her hands on some salt. Leaning over the pot, she breathed deeply. She couldn't remember when last she had smelled real meat boiling in their tenement.

In a festive mood, she switched the tune and continued to hum contentedly as she swept the floor with half an old scrubbing brush. Gail had continued gathering posies, but darkness was just starting to fall in the west; it wouldn't be long before she and Papa were both home. Abbie couldn't wait to see their faces when she presented them with real beef broth. Maybe Papa would even bring them some bread to go with it.

She opened the door and swept the dust out into the hallway, then up to the front door, wishing for a dustpan. When she pulled the front door open, shock rippled through her.

She had been so busy cooking that she hadn't even thought about how dark it was outside.

Her heart thumped painfully against her chest as she stared out into the street. Streetlights were few and far between here, and they were still the old oil lantern types, their yellow light flickering and sickly as it struggled in vain to hold back the tide of night. The sky was absolutely pitch black; there was no moon, nor a single star, all veiled behind the lowering clouds.

And there was no sign of Gail.

Abbie felt fear rise in her like nausea. A thousand warnings crowded into her mind, each more dire than the last. *The wharves are a dangerous place. So many things can happen to you.* Repeated in the voices of Papa and Patrick, they filled her until it felt like her heart and lungs were being squeezed. She thought of the grocer's hateful expression. She thought of the way some of the young men would look at them when they walked past.

Abbie took a step forward, ready to rush into the streets and look for her sister, then hesitated. What would Papa say if he knew she was rushing off into the dark? He would be furious. But Gail was out there. Or maybe she'd just walked over to the spot where Papa was always hawking his fish, and maybe they were coming home together. Abbie wanted to lean into the thought and relax, but her heart was still hammering. *What if they weren't?* What if Gail was out there all alone?

She couldn't bear it. She had to go find her; Papa would understand, and as for the perils out there in the dark, they were nothing compared to her fear for her sister.

Pausing to grab her threadbare coat from inside the tenement, Abbie took the pot off the fire and hurried out into the streets, praying silently that Gail would soon be home and able to enjoy the meal Abbie was making.

She walked quickly, the collar of her coat drawn up to her cheekbones, avoiding the shadows as much as she could. The journey to the spot where Papa always sold fish wasn't a long one – only about twenty minutes' walk – but in the darkness it felt like an eternity. Abbie hurried from streetlight to streetlight, her heart pounding in her throat anytime she stepped into the darkness.

It was dark, but the city was a long way from sleeping. All around Abbie, the sounds of a London night were growing in strength. There were bursts of music and coarse laughter from the odd public house that she passed. Cats howled and fought in the shadows; whenever she passed a quiet alley, Abbie heard the skittering of tiny claws on the ground as rats fled from her noisy presence. Rocking, mumbling figures bundled in rags reached out pale, thin hands toward her when she passed.

Abbie hated the sounds from the handful of brothels she passed more than anything else. She clapped her hands over her ears, feeling the evil surrounding those places as though it were something physical slithering across her skin, and broke into a jog.

Even though she was leaving the worst of the slum behind as she hurried to the park, Abbie was well aware that the danger was by no means over. Still, it felt good to be reaching streets populated by horses and carriages rather than slinking, shadowy figures on foot. Carriage lights made it easier to stay out of the shadows.

She was just starting to think she might reach Papa unscathed when she heard the scream.

It was a terrible, hoarse, animal sound of total fear and agony, sobbing and sharp, and it stopped Abbie dead in her tracks. She froze, her heart thundering against her ribs. *Gail.* But the cry was too deep, even it in its panicked pitch, to be female.

Everything in Abbie screamed for her to go home. But then she heard the pleading, sobbing voice.

"Please. Please. Don't kill me. I'll pay you. I'll get you the money. I can't do that if I'm dead, can I? I'll – ahh."

It was cut off short in a gasp of fear and agony. Abbie couldn't keep her back to it. She turned around, took a step forward, and spotted two shadowy figures in an alley nearby.

Traffic continued to rattle past as if nothing untoward was happening. Perhaps the people in the carriages couldn't hear the man's screams; at any rate, none of them slowed down. There was just one horse standing near the mouth of the alley, leaning back uncertainly against its reins, which were tied tightly to a lamppost.

But though the figures were wreathed in shadow, Abbie could hear the terrified sobs of the one pressed up against the wall. A taller figure stood over him, and she saw the glint of a knife.

"You've been saying that for months, you insolent fool," hissed a second voice. It was clipped and polished, well educated. "I trusted you at first. But now, like an ignorant hornswoggler, you've sold all my opium and gambled away *my* profits. And now you're going to pay for it with the only thing you have left." The knife flashed, and the victim let out a muffled cry of pain. "Your wretched, miserable life."

"Please," the victim begged. "Please. You wouldn't kill an unarmed man, would you? Would you?"

"I've done worse," hissed the man with the knife.

"I have a wife. Children," gasped the victim.

The man with the knife gave a sardonic chuckle. "They'll be better off without you." He raised the knife.

It flashed dazzlingly, and Abbie saw the silvery glint of its deadly edge, and her throat closed with horror and nausea. She lunged forward, light cascading down over her as she stepped under a different streetlamp.

"No!" she cried.

The word was drowned out by a terrible, gargling sound that came from the victim. Abbie saw the knife plunge into his throat. There was a gush of dark fluid, and a horrible, jerking movement from the man with the knife. The victim's gurgling cry was cut off short. He slithered to the ground and half-sat, half-lay there, blood surging out onto his lap, twitching unnaturally.

Abbie could neither move nor breathe. She had seen dead people before and even the possibly fatal result of a few street fights, but she had never seen someone killed. Never seen so much blood.

Then the man with the knife tossed the weapon aside and stepped out into the street, glancing left and right. And in the light that fell from the streetlamp, Abbie looked directly into the eyes of a murderer.

They were palest grey, almost white, set in a strong, chiseled face. Abbie saw every detail: the angry arch of the pale brows, the moon whiteness of the skin, the long blond ponytail tied at the nape of the man's neck. She saw his high cheekbones and the way the streetlight cast shadows underneath them, sharp as the slant of the knife he had hidden underneath his coat. It was a well-cut coat, finely tailored, dark blue; a golden chain glinted at his chest pocket. She saw the thin lips, the smirk lifting the corner of his mouth, as though the life that was seeping out of the throat of the man in the alley had not been worth more than the pleasure he'd had in taking it.

And, most terrifying of all, Abbie saw him see her.

Their eyes locked. She was suddenly and terribly aware of the fact that she was standing directly beneath a gas lamp, and that its yellow light was shining on her as brilliantly as the next lamp was shining on the killer. He knew she had witnessed everything, and his eyes narrowed. His hand went to his coat.

Abbie didn't have the breath to scream. She simply turned and fled, her body burning with fear, adrenalin coursing through her as she bolted. Reaching the end of the street, she spotted a dark alley to her left; the shadows that had felt so dangerous moments before now felt like refuge. She flung herself into it, pressing her back to the wall, her heart hammering uncontrollably.

It was almost impossible to hear anything over the wild pounding of her heart, but after several moments, Abbie realised there were no footsteps chasing her. The man hadn't come after her.

Sobbing with fear, Abbie crumpled to the ground, covering her mouth with her hands to keep her choked breaths quiet. She had just seen a man killed. She had just seen his life taken.

And worst of all, the murderer had seen Abbie.

She wished with all of her heart to forget his face, to forget the terrible sound of the dying man, but she knew it was burned into her memory with a fierce, vivid harshness that she would never forget. The look that had come into the murderer's eyes when he realised she'd seen him terrified her. It wasn't a look of dismay or shock. It was a predatory look, almost satisfied, as if he were pleased that he now had someone else to kill.

She had no doubt that he would plunge that same knife into her soon, if he thought she could identify him.

Fleetingly, Abbie thought of the police. They seldom came down here to the wharves, but she knew she'd find them easily if she ventured toward the marketplaces. Then she remembered the way that the policeman had looked at her just days ago, the contempt in his eyes. Who would believe a poor girl like her, compared with that well-dressed young gentleman?

She had to run. She had to get back to the tenement before he came after her. But she couldn't stop thinking of that poor man with the cut throat, of the terrible sound he had made. He'd still been twitching when she fled. Maybe the killer had left. Maybe the man was still alive and suffering. Could she help him?

The thought drove her to her feet. She had to find out if the man was still alive.

Trembling from head to foot, Abbie peered out of the alley. The street was quiet; not a soul stirred, except for a rat watching her from the top of a wall with beady eyes, a piece of garbage clutched in its little pink paws. Abbie stepped out of the alley on wobbling legs and made her way to the street corner. She peeked around the corner nervously.

There was no sign of the killer, but a crowd had already gathered around the mouth of the alley. People were talking, gesticulating, looking around with wide, horrified eyes. Carriages stopped, traffic piling up. Somewhere, a policeman's whistle sounded.

Abbie could see nothing of the victim except for the great pool of blood lying on the sidewalk. The killer, too, seemed to have disappeared.

"Is he dead?" cried a horrified voice from the crowd.

There was a moment's silence. Then, a leaden voice. "Yes."

Tears stung Abbie's eyes. She darted back into her alleyway and pressed the heels of her hands to her temples, breathing in ragged, shallow gasps. It was true, then. She had seen a murder. She had seen a man killed and looked directly into the face of his killer… and he knew.

Even hidden in the shadows of the alley, Abbie had the terrible feeling that she was glowing bright red, that she had the word "TARGET" stamped across her forehead.

She took deep breaths, trying to calm herself, and a rational thought finally entered her mind. She couldn't tell Papa or Gail. If they knew, they would be in just as much danger as she was. She had to keep this a secret.

Gail. Abbie had almost forgotten she had set out to find her sister. A fresh wave of fear washed through her. Papa was right; the streets were dangerous in the dark, so much more dangerous than Abbie had ever imagined. She had to find her sister. Or was the killer out there somewhere, ready to follow her? Would she lead him straight to her family?

And if she went home, would she lead him straight home?

She didn't know what to do, but she had to make sure her father and Gail never found out about what had happened. She would have to go home. She would have to pretend she had never been out on these streets in the dark, or Papa would ask if she was all right, and she would cry and cry – and he would find out. She could never let that happen.

In tears of panic, Abbie did the only thing that she could think of doing. She ran straight home.

ABBIE HAD BARELY REACHED the house, started the fire, and started warming up the broth again when she heard the front door creak.

Crouched by the fire, she held her breath for a moment. She had managed to dry her tears, and although her chest ached from running, she could no longer feel the panicked hammering of her heart. Still, every time she closed her eyes, even to blink, she saw the man dying in the alley.

But when she recognized Papa's footsteps on hallway, she closed her eyes tightly, praying with all of her heart that a second set of footsteps would come through that door. A second later, they did. Tears of relief stung her eyes. Gail was with him after all.

The door swung open, and Abbie swallowed her tears quickly, straightening up. She didn't have to fake the relief that filled her tone as Papa and Gail walked in, both looking tired and pale, but whole and healthy.

"Gail," she gasped. "There you are. I've been so worried."

She couldn't stop herself from rushing up to her sister and throwing her arms around her, hugging her tightly to her chest. Fear lanced through her belly. Had she done the right thing to come home? Had she placed her treasured sister in danger? She couldn't forgive herself if something happened to Gail, and she felt sick to her stomach, clutching her a little tighter.

"I'm fine, Abbie." Gail wriggled out of Abbie's grip, looking surprised. "I just walked home with Papa, that's all."

Papa kissed Abbie on the cheek as he limped into the room. "I'm sorry, darling," he said. "I told Gail she'd frighten the life out of you."

Abbie knew she was dangerously close to giving herself away. She took a shaky breath, trying to calm herself, and forced a smile.

"I'm sorry," said Gail. "I thought you'd just assume I went with Papa."

"It's all right," said Abbie, forcing a light tone. She turned away quickly. "The broth's nearly ready."

"I just didn't want to be caught on the streets alone in the dark," said Gail. "I thought I might not make it home, so I went to find Papa instead."

"You made the right choice," said Abbie. A terrible shudder ran through her whole body. "The streets are an awful, awful place in the dark."

She straightened up to fetch the bowls for the broth, and Papa was right in front of her. His eyes locked with hers, and he laid a hand on her cheek. His touch was so warm and tender that it almost broke her. Concern filled his expression.

"Are you all right, Abbie dear?" he said.

"Yes," said Abbie, forcing a smile. "I'm just fine, Papa." She pulled her face away and bent over the pot on the fire. "Now, I think we all need some nice, hot supper."

Gail and Papa didn't argue, and Abbie breathed for what felt like the first time in hours. Maybe, just maybe, she would be able to keep the two of them safe after all.

CHAPTER 3

THE SUNSHINE WAS UNSEASONABLY warm and bright, but it did nothing to reassure Abbie as she and Gail made their way through the slum toward the marketplace, each carrying a basket of posies. She kept her eyes wide open, feeling half blind and deaf as she glanced left and right into every shadow.

It had been three days since she had seen the murder. The sound of the dying man's last breath and the dark colour of his blood as it had flowed onto the sidewalk continued to plague her every night. The murderer stalked through her dreams, always wearing that cocksure sneer, his knife always ready in his hand.

There was no escaping him at night, and even in the daytime, Abbie feared she would see him around the corner at any moment. As she and Gail crossed another muddy street, she spotted a tall, older tramp on a street corner, leaning against the door of a rickety tenement building. His eyes rested on her as she walked past, and her heart thumped painfully against her ribs. Was he just staring in the way men always stared? Or did he know the murderer? Had he been told to look out for a scruffy young girl with red hair and brown eyes?

"Hello? Abbie?" said Gail sharply.

Abbie jumped, realizing that Gail had been talking to her. "Sorry," she said. "What was that?"

"I said, where do you want us to go today?" said Gail impatiently. "We haven't sold many posies in the last few days, so we have to do better. Shall we try the market square down by the wharves today?"

Abbie considered it. She didn't want to be seen anywhere near the wharves. "I have an idea," she said. "Why don't you go to the wharves, and I'll try up near the park? We'll meet up again at the crossroads before dark."

A stubborn, pouty expression crossed Gail's pretty little face. "You want us to split up again?" she said. "I thought we were supposed to take care of each other."

I'm trying my best to take care of you, Abbie thought. She mustered a smile. "Well, I think you're starting to get old enough to hold your own," she said. "You're not a tiny little girl anymore, are you, Gail?"

Her attempt at distraction worked. Gail's mouth curved up in a proud smile, happy to be called an adult, as any twelve-year-old girl would be. "I guess not," she said.

"See? You'll do great. Maybe we can make more money this way," Abbie said.

"All right. Let's do that," said Gail.

They had reached the crossroads leading deeper into the city. The girls both stopped, and Gail gave Abbie a wide, happy smile, almost as bright as the little posies gleaming in her basket, the delicate flowers slightly wilted yet still brilliantly colourful.

"See you tonight, then," said Gail.

"Yes." Abbie smiled, willing it to be true. "I'll see you."

"All right. Have a good day." Gail grinned and turned to go, and Abbie watched her little sister marching off with determination, her long ponytails swinging over her shabby dress. She felt a surge of desperation to hold onto what she had. Sometimes there wasn't enough food and sometimes the rent was late, but she would give anything for her father and her little sister, anything in the world.

"Gail," she called, on an impulse.

Gail turned around. "Yes?" she said.

Abbie raised her voice above the morning traffic. "I love you!" she shouted.

Gail looked a little startled, but her smile bounced back even brighter than before. "I love you, too," she called, and then went skipping off again.

Abbie squeezed her eyes tight shut. *See you tonight*, she repeated in her heart. It had to be true.

She didn't know what she would do without them.

As always for this time of morning, the roads and sidewalks were almost equally hectic. Hansom-cabs went swirling around corners and storming down streets, darting in and out among omnibuses and horsemen. Pedestrians dashed across the street at odd moments, making cab drivers curse dreadfully. Among it all, little boys with flat caps and shovels dove in among the churning legs of the horses and the spinning wheels of the carts, scooping up the road apples that lay inevitably everywhere in steaming piles. They got paid by the pile, yet they risked their lives for every penny.

Abbie didn't have time to watch the little boys this morning. She walked quickly, her head low, bonnet pulled down on her forehead, basket on her arm. The more space she put between herself and the wharves, the better.

She was desperate, too, not to be seen out in public with Gail. As much as it frightened her to send her little sister off alone, she had to make sure Gail was safe.

For the umpteenth time that morning, she glanced over her shoulder. It was impossible to tell, in the crush of people, if she was being followed; but for a moment, her eyes met those of a gaunt-faced man with a shock of dirty white hair, walking among the crowd, his hands thrust deep into his coat pockets. Their gazes locked for an instant, and then he dropped his eyes casually, looking around.

Abbie walked a little faster, her skin crawling. Had he been watching her? Had it simply been a coincidence that their eyes met at that moment?

There was a side street off to her left, and Abbie turned sharply down it, still walking quickly. There were only a few people walking down this street, and a single cart stood on the corner, a skinny horse drooping in the shafts. She held her breath for a few yards, then looked back again.

The man with the white hair had just turned down the same street.

Abbie's heart thumped hard. Over the past few days, she'd constantly suspected that she was being followed, but this was the first time that her suspicions had come true. Panic seized her. Clutching her basket of posies, she broke into a jog.

Behind her, the man did the same thing.

Abbie knew that screaming would be useless. No one listened to screams in this part of London. She threw down the basket and bolted and heard the thump of feet as the man pursued. Her heart raced in her ears, her breath stinging in her lungs as she bolted. There was a curve at the end of the street. Maybe it led back to the main street, maybe she could rush back out there and get lost in the crowd –

Abbie made the turn as fast as she could, grabbing at a lamp-post, and jolted forward, but there was no main street here. Just a dead end, a brick wall straight ahead, tenement doors to her right and left. And standing in the street just a few yards away, the man with the pale eyes and the smirk.

She skidded to a halt. He smiled at her, and it made her skin crawl.

"Oh, there you are," he purred. "We've been looking for you, little miss." He reached into his coat and pulled out his knife. The edge gleamed dully in the morning light.

Abbie looked over her shoulder. The white-haired man was blocking the street behind her.

"There's nowhere to run, you little street wench," said the man with the knife. He took a slow, low pace toward her, prowling like a predator. His eyes were gleaming. Abbie could only think of the dead man's thick, dark blood pooling on the ground. She remembered the way he had gurgled. The tattered edges of the wound in his neck.

"Please," she whimpered, the word coming out on a burst of terrified tears. "Please, my family needs me. I won't tell a soul. Not a soul. I haven't even told them."

"You know I can't take that chance." The man raised the knife. "And why would I want to?" He licked his lips.

There was a door to Abbie's left, and it was her only hope. The man took a step nearer, and with a despairing cry, Abbie threw herself sideways and kicked open the door. It slammed back on its hinges and she bolted into a dark hallway, tripping and stumbling over things – over people lying in the hall. A chorus of angry yells pursued her, and she heard the man with the knife shouting, and she just kept running.

She felt, rather than saw, empty space through a doorway on her left. With a gasp of panic, Abbie flung herself through the door and ducked into a dark corner, clapping her hand over her mouth and nose. Nothing moved inside; the room was so dark and windowless that she could see nothing except for the faint outline of sunlight against a doorway on the opposite side. It could be a storeroom. It could be filled with people. It could be filled with snakes; Abbie didn't know.

She didn't care at that moment, either, keeping her hand over her face to muffle her panicked breathing as she listened to the feet of her pursuers race nearer and nearer. The first set of footsteps charged straight past. The second passed the doorway and stopped, and Abbie held her breath. Her traitorous heart was thumping so hard in her chest that she felt certain the man must be able to hear it.

She listened to his heavy breathing, her lungs burning for air, allowing herself tiny sips to avoid gasping out loud.

After a few moments, slower footsteps returned.

"Lawrence?" said the voice of the pale-eyed man with the knife. "Did you get her?" He spoke calmly, as if "getting" Abbie was some simple, innocuous act.

"No, guv," said the white-haired man's voice. "She's gone."

"She can't be *gone*," spat the pale-eyed man. "She's somewhere in here, in this den of opium." He raised his voice, and Abbie heard his feet pacing closer. "I know you're in here," he called out, his voice playful, sing-song. "I know you can hear me. I think it would be best for you to come out now."

Abbie closed her eyes tightly as the footsteps paused in the doorway, mere inches from her. The darkness was absolute.

A slow, velvet chuckle slid down Abbie's spine like a snake.

"All right, then. Hide," he purred. "That makes for much better sport." The footsteps turned and went back into the hall; Abbie let out a tiny breath, too scared to move. "Search the place, Lawrence, room by room," said the pale-eyed man. "But when you find her, don't kill her. Bring her to me."

The implication made tears of fear run down Abbie's cheeks.

"And block off the doors first," the pale-eyed man added.

Abbie looked up at the outline of the doorway etched against the darkness on the opposite side of the room. It was her only chance, and she had to take it now, before the white-haired man closed it off. She leaned forward, placing her bare hands against the floor. It was grimy and sticky; small objects rattled against her fingers, some of them feeling sharp. She had no other choice. She began to crawl, slowly, placing her hands and knees with terrible care to avoid making a single sound. And all the while, she could hear the two men moving around in the hallway behind her.

She was getting closer. It was hard to guess the distance in the darkness, but she knew she was nearly there; she could feel the draft on her face coming from beneath the door. She reached out, but instead of finding the rough wooden surface of the door, her fingers bumped into something smooth and cold.

Something that tipped and shattered deafeningly on the floor.

"There!" roared the voice of the pale-eyed man. "There she is."

Abbie lunged to her feet, panicking. Her shoes crunched on shattered clay, but her hands found a doorknob. It squeaked, and for an awful moment, Abbie thought the door was locked. The men's footsteps were right behind her. She flung the door open, sunlight dazzling her eyes, and a hand grabbed the back of her dress, gripping it with terrifying strength. Abbie twisted, screaming at the top of her lungs, and with a ripping sound she broke free and bolted into the street.

"Look out!" bellowed an angry voice, and suddenly Abbie's world was filled with hooves; a man on horseback clung on determinedly as the horse she'd startled danced on its hindlegs, shoes flashing in the sun. She ducked underneath its belly and ran directly into the street. There was a yell of frustration from behind her.

"Chase her!" roared the pale-eyed man. "Don't let her get away."

Abbie ducked around a racing hansom, bolted in front of a grocer's wagon to curses from the drivers.

"I'll find you!" roared the pale-eyed man. "I'll find you, and when I do, I'll kill you. I'll kill you and all your family."

Fear lent wings to Abbie's feet then. She glanced over her shoulder and saw the white-haired man was close behind. And even though she wanted nothing more than to run home, she knew she couldn't.

Perhaps she never could again.

She ducked down the first side street she could find and kept running, pushing over garbage cans, pushing aside pedestrians, ducking around horses and carts with tears streaming down her cheeks. But wherever she ran, the white-haired man was close behind.

CHAPTER 4

When Abbie finally slowed, it was not so much because of a certainty that the men were no longer following her than because she could run not another step.

She had no idea where she was. Her panicked flight had brought her down so many streets and through so many different districts that she had become completely disoriented. The city that was her only home now seemed like a hostile wasteland. There were buildings all around her, a maze of them, all of them shadowy, with dusty windows and cobwebs in the eaves. The rank smell of unwashed humanity filled every breath that Abbie took.

She stumbled into a narrow alley, littered with the bones of small animals and puddles that shimmered with filth, and collapsed with her back to a plain wall only one brick thick. Head between her knees, Abbie sobbed and cried and gasped for breath, every muscle in her body burning helplessly.

It took several moments for her heart and breathing to slow down to the point where Abbie could hear anything else beyond her own body. She leaned her head back against the filthy wall, sucking in deep, desperate breaths. The beady eyes of a rat watched her from its hiding spot behind a garbage can. Beyond the alley, people were moving to and fro, avoiding the litter that was everywhere.

But no one came rushing into the alley. No white-haired thug or knife-wielding gentleman burst inside to gut her like a fish.

Abbie wiped at her tears with the back of a grimy hand, reality slowly sinking in. She'd lost them. Somehow, she had escaped from the men.

But now she had no idea where she was. She rose shakily to her feet and wobbled to the mouth of the alley, staring up and down a grubby street. A stall made from rags and sticks drooped on the corner, like hers and Gail's always did, but this one belonged to a toothless old woman stirring a pot of gruel. There was a fish shop and a butchery that smelled rancid; a public house; a seedy-looking building with frilly pink curtains in the windows that were not boarded up. There was no sign over its door.

Abbie tried to remember which way she had run. She knew she had turned her back toward her home and bolted. She must be closer to the centre of London now; she knew she could find her way back, if she turned her face toward the river and kept going in the direction of the wharves.

She took a step forward, then halted, terror rushing through her as she remembered the words of the pale-eyed man.

I'll kill you and all your family.

Abbie's heart thumped. What would happen if she went home? How long had the white-haired man been following her today? Had he seen her with Gail? Did he know she had a little sister with guileless eyes and a pretty smile? Did he know she had a crippled father with a tender voice?

She didn't know the answer, but she did know that if she returned to the wharves, there would always be men to follow her. The gentleman killer had more than enough money to hire all the thugs he wanted to follow Abbie around. Sooner or later, they would find her family.

She remembered the gurgling sound the victim had made as he died, and a brief, awful image of Papa and Gail, their throats slit open and blood cascading to the ground, flashed through her mind.

"No." Abbie gasped, clapping her hands over her eyes as if that could block out her thoughts. "No... no, no, no no."

She was trembling all over. She wanted, with everything in her, to go back home, to wrap her arms around Gail and bury herself in Papa's warm embrace.

But she couldn't. She could never go home again, or she would endanger Papa and Gail forever.

Sobs claimed Abbie once more, and she sank to the ground, her arms wrapped around her chest as if that could keep all the broken pieces of her heart from flying away.

ABBIE ONLY MOVED when it began to rain.

She wasn't sure when the clouds had come over the city; she had spent most of the day curled up in the alley, too exhausted to move, sleeping in fitful bursts despite the smells, sounds, and sights that surrounded her. All she could think of was Papa and Gail, of how confused and heartbroken they would be when she never returned. Would they search for her? Would Gail cry?

Would Papa cry?

The thought sent a fresh rush of tears down her cheeks, but the rain washed them away, pounding on her face, so cold that it numbed her skin. Summer had not quite come to the city yet, and the rain still felt like winter. In moments, Abbie was soaked to the skin. Her aching muscles started to shiver, and she realised that she was hungrier and thirstier than she had ever been in her life.

In her heart, Abbie just wanted to stay in the alley, curled up, and accept whatever fate came to her. But her instincts forced her to her feet. Food. Water. Shelter. She needed those three things. That was a fact she could focus on, something concrete and simple to distract her from her heartache.

She stumbled into the street and gazed listlessly left and right, trying to decide which way to go. Even the rancid scent coming from the butchery made her mouth water now, but she had no money. She had thrown everything aside in her panicked flight from the men.

She needed money. For that she had to do one of three things: steal, beg, or work. Her thoughts dripped through her mind with the crystal clarity of a body bent on nothing but survival. She was too old to beg. She was no good at stealing. She had to find work.

Ignoring the crush of rising traffic around her, Abbie staggered forward. There was a bakery just down the street; rough rye breads and sacks of flour were displayed in its windows. Maybe she could sweep their floors or wash their windows and make a few pennies, enough to buy a cup of water and a little bread...

"I wouldn't go there if I was you, luv."

Abbie stopped, gazing around for the source of the voice. She was standing just opposite the building with the frilly curtains, and a woman in her forties was leaning against the door, smoking a pipe. Abbie had never seen a woman smoke before. She stared in vague surprise as the woman blew out a thin stream of grey smoke.

"That baker's no good," said the woman. She tugged at the front of her corset, which swooped lower than Abbie was comfortable with. "Set his dogs on you, he will."

Abbie stared at the woman, who sucked at her pipe again. Her face was so powdered, and her cheeks so rouged, that it was impossible to tell what her skin tone was really like. But despite the gold and silver paint around her eyes, when Abbie looked into them, she could still see a soul toughened by hardship.

"I don't know what else to do," said Abbie. "I'm so hungry." She didn't know if she trusted this woman, but it was the first time all day that she felt like someone could actually see her. As though she weren't invisible.

"Go home, then," said the woman. "Look at your dress. You're not out on the streets, are you?"

"No," said Abbie. "But I can never go home." She allowed the tears to flow unchecked down her cheeks. "I can never go home again."

The woman blew another puff of smoke, watching Abbie with calculating eyes, yet they held a hint of softness in them. "What's your name, luv?" she asked.

"Abbie."

"You're a pretty little thing." She sighed, rising to her feet. "I know what it's like to have a home you can't go back to. Wait right here."

Abbie did so, hardly knowing why, as the woman disappeared into the building. She returned a few moments later, this time accompanied by a much older lady of awe-inspiring proportions. Abbie didn't think it possible that someone with so many chins could have such a tiny waist, nipped in and down by a tightly drawn corset. Her bosom wobbled majestically as she strutted up to Abbie on heeled shoes.

"What's this then, Priscilla?" she demanded, giving Abbie a critical look. "You know we have no use for a foundling."

"Just look at her a minute, Lady Rose," said Priscilla impatiently. She took a puff on her pipe.

"I've told you not to smoke that thing," said Lady Rose. "You'll put off the customers. They're not after a woman who smells like an ashtray."

"I'll put on some perfume," said Priscilla, putting the pipe aside, nonetheless. "She'll make a fine lady for you, ma'am. Look at those eyes."

Lady Rose gave Abbie a long, assessing look from bottom to top. She felt like a piece of fruit at the market, being felt and turned over by careless fingers.

"How old are you?" she demanded.

"Fourteen, ma'am," Abbie stammered.

"Much too young to be a lady of the night," Lady Rose scoffed.

Abbie felt a jolt of horror. She backed away. "I don't want to do that," she gasped.

"You see?" Lady Rose shook her head. "Don't waste my time, Priscilla. Get rid of that pipe. And hitch your skirts a little higher, do. The men like to see some ankles."

Lady Rose started moving through the door, and Abbie saw the inside of the building for the first time. It was more colourful and opulent, all drapes and curtains and carpets, than she liked; but a delicious whiff of food floated through the open door, and Abbie could have cried with hunger.

"No, please," she gasped, hurrying up to Lady Rose. "Please, don't go. I can work for you."

"You're too young," snapped Lady Rose.

"But I can do... other things," said Abbie. "I can cook and clean and sew. I'll wash your floors and mend your clothing and cook your food... please..." She swallowed a sob.

Lady Rose gave her a long, appraising stare.

"Please, Lady Rose," Priscilla said, her voice much smaller and quieter than it was before. "She's going to starve out here."

"Thousands of waifs starve in London," said Lady Rose sharply. "Do you think they're my problem, Priscilla?"

"No, but I do know that we've been short on women since Cookie left," said Priscilla. "That's not good for business, is it?"

Lady Rose glanced at Priscilla, then let out a sigh, looking back at Abbie.

"Fine," she said. "But don't expect to be paid, girl. It remains to be seen if you'll even be worth the scraps from our table."

"Oh, thank you." Abbie's knees buckled, and she fell to the grubby sidewalk in front of the brothel, tears of gratitude streaming down her cheeks. "Thank you, ma'am, thank you."

Lady Rose had already disappeared back into the building. Priscilla crouched down and grabbed Abbie's arm, pulling her to her feet.

"Chin up, girl," she said. "Things could be worse for you."

She let out a quiet sigh. "They could be worse for all of us."

PART II

CHAPTER 5

Two Years Later

Abbie had never meant to stay at the brothel for longer than a few days.

She sat outside in the back alley, enjoying a rare burst of spring sunshine as she worked on the dress draped over her knees. One of the men had been rough with Daisy the night before, and there was a tear in the sleeve. Abbie tried not to think about the fear that had filled Daisy's scream as it resounded through the brothel last night, or about the terrible look in the eyes of the man whom Lady Rose had hauled bodily out of Daisy's room, practically kicking him down the stairs. Daisy had cried and cried.

Abbie made another neat little stitch, tying it off with a practiced movement. She had mended so many of these dresses over the last two years that their garish colours and swooping necklines no longer surprised her. Daisy had always been cruel to Abbie, but she had felt sorry for her when she served breakfast that morning and found the usually stern and tight-lipped woman sitting hunched at the end of the table, staring at nothing. She had pushed her eggs around her plate without interest. The novelty of Abbie's good cooking had worn off since she first arrived two years ago.

Abbie finished the last stitch in the dress, pressed her needle into a pincushion, and lifted the dress. Its gaudy green colour caught the sunlight and sparkled. She tried to admire the neat row of stitches she had made, and not to look at the cut of the dress, at the straps and garters. Even now, it still turned her stomach. Her room was in the basement, and she was grateful for it. She didn't want to hear the nightly sounds of the brothel.

She shook her head. She didn't want to think about it; it was the only way she could live with the fact that the brothel had now become her home. At least, she told herself gratefully as she rose to her feet and tucked the dress over her arm, she herself was still so young and slim that the customers never even gave her a second glance. She would rather scrub floors and cook meals for the rest of her life than spend one night plying that trade.

She walked into the brothel kitchen to find two of the ladies gathered around the table. Daisy was not among them; Abbie was mostly relieved to see. Priscilla, the older lady who had helped Abbie to get her job here in the first place, was sitting at the head of the table as usual. The girl sitting on her right, clutching both of Priscilla's hands and crying hopelessly, was only a little older than Abbie herself.

"Stop that noise, pet," said Priscilla, firmly but not unkindly. "You'll spoil your face, and Lady Rose will be upset."

"It's just so awful," sobbed the new girl. "I hate it here."

"So do I. So do all of us," said Priscilla, "but what can we do? Do you think it would be better out on the streets? At least here we're fed and paid." She touched the girl's chin. "Sally, stop crying and listen to me."

Sally sniffed and swallowed her tears, raising a tear-streaked face to Priscilla. The older woman's tone was gentle.

"Why aren't you home with your family?" she asked quietly.

Sally lowered her eyes. "Things were good once," she said. "Papa left when we were little children, but Mama was always good to us. Then the consumption took her. My brother went off to war. My little sister drowned in the Thames, God rest her soul, grubbing in the mud for bits of coal..." A fresh rush of tears glittered down Sally's cheeks. "I went to live with my uncle. I thought he'd be good to me." She looked up at Priscilla and swallowed hard. "Not a day went by that he didn't beat me, and worse."

"Now see, Sally," said Priscilla calmly, "this is better. Lady Rose doesn't beat us like some of her kind do."

"I just don't know if I can bear it," said Sally tearfully.

"You have to bear it," said Priscilla. "Just keep your chin up. Your heart will harden. You just have to let it."

Abbie felt her own heart breaking at Priscilla's words as she turned to the pot on the stove, which bubbled full of potatoes for the ladies' supper. She picked up a fork and prodded one of the potatoes with it, wondering what she would have done if Priscilla hadn't begged Lady Rose to hire Abbie as a sort of housekeeper for the brothel. Would she have given in? Would it be her crying to Priscilla now? She ran a hand down the front of her dress, grateful for her tiny, malnourished figure.

"So now stop that fuss," said Priscilla. "You'll be all right. Won't she, Abbie? Go on – tell her she'll be all right."

Abbie turned around and met Sally's eyes. What she saw there terrified her. They were so hollow, so filled with utter hopelessness. She must have been pretty once, Abbie thought, when her parents were still alive; she had sweetly rounded cheeks, and wide, blue eyes that might have looked angelic if they were not so reddened with tears. Her makeup was smeared all over her face, and the curls that Lady Rose had forced into her hair with a curling iron were coming undone and frizzing.

Abbie thought of how Daisy had cried, of the bloodstains she had washed out of the older woman's dress. She couldn't tell Sally that she would be all right, and despite the safety of the four walls around her, she felt a familiar panic deep in her belly. Even after two years, Abbie still felt trapped.

"We're having bangers and mash for supper," she said, trying to keep her voice as light and happy as possible. "I'll make some lovely gravy, and I'm sure there are still some peas, too."

Sally hung her head. Abbie turned back to the pot, knowing that she had failed.

***

ALTHOUGH ABBIE FOUND MOST of her work quite pleasant, it was cleaning the entrance hall that she hated the most. Everything about it had an opulent, suggestive feeling to it that made her want to wash her hands the moment she stepped onto the sickly lime-green carpet. The curtains had huge, heavy purple drapes that were always drawn; there were feathers everywhere, and fake flowers made from fabric, and paintings of Renaissance women with their robes hanging dangerously low and their dark eyes wide. A staircase led up to the rooms.

Abbie tried not to look around at any of it. Sitting by the wooden counter where Lady Rose held court in the evenings, she focused on the task at hand: polishing the wood. Working her cloth back and forth over the wood, she looked down at her reflection in the bright surface, wondering if Papa and Gail would recognize her. What would Papa think of her working at a place like this?

She wished she could see them. In the past years, she had grown oriented to where the brothel was in relation to the rest of London, and she knew she could easily find her way back home. There were times – times when the ladies cursed at her, and Lady Rose left only scraps for her to eat – that she considered going back.

A deep sigh escaped her, and she hung her head, closing her eyes against the looming tears. She knew she couldn't go back. She knew, from how deeply they had all always missed Patrick, that Papa and Gail had been missing her. She even hoped they would forgive her somehow for leaving them. But the thought of the pale-eyed man with the knife still kept her from returning to the family she adored. She hadn't seen him for years, except in her nightmares, where he still visited her every time she closed her eyes.

She knew it was possible that he had lost her, or that he had forgotten all about it. Perhaps he would have killed her by now if he really wanted to. But she could not bear the thought of leading him back to her family, and each time she considered it, she heard the gurgling sound of that stranger dying in a pool of his own blood.

When she opened her eyes and looked down into the counter, a second face was looking up at her in the reflection. Abbie jumped, spinning around. Lady Rose was standing there, a cigarette dangling between her fingers, dripping ash onto the carpet that Abbie had just cleaned.

"I don't feed you just so that you can fall asleep while you work, child," Lady Rose rasped.

Abbie swallowed hard. "No, ma'am," she said. "I... I was just..."

"I don't want to hear it." Lady Rose waved a hand, smoke tracing the movement. "Finish polishing that and then go to the kitchen. I've ordered a delivery of flour, and I want you to be there to make sure it's in order."

"Yes, ma'am," said Abbie.

Lady Rose studied her the way she often did, her assessing look traveling up and down Abbie's body, like she was a piece of furniture that the pimp was thinking of buying.

"You're a little scrap of a thing, aren't you?" she sighed on a cloud of smoke. "Well, at least you make good food." She waved a hand. "Go on, then."

Abbie obediently turned back to the counter and resumed her polishing as Lady Rose swept out and the door swung shut behind her. There were moments when Lady Rose could show a tiny breath of softness, yet most of the time, she was the most terrifying thing that Abbie had ever seen.

As soon as she had finished polishing the counter, Abbie gathered up her cleaning supplies and hurried down to the kitchen. She was surprised to find the kitchen empty. Usually, the kitchen table was a gathering point for many of the ladies, who spent most of their mornings asleep and their afternoons sitting around with expressions of deep exhaustion on their faces. They often sat around the table and talked or drank or smoked. Abbie disliked the two latter activities, but she knew it was the only time to relax that these ladies ever had.

She headed to the cupboard in the back of the kitchen to put away her basket of cleaning supplies and had nearly reached it when there was a clatter from the pantry. Hesitating, Abbie looked over at the pantry door. It was closed, as usual, and for a second, she thought she had imagined the sound.

Still... Abbie shuddered. Not long ago, there had been an enormous rat in there, and it had torn a great hole in a bag of sugar and spilled it all over the floor. Lady Rose had been extremely angry.

Reaching into the cupboard, Abbie grasped her best broom. Holding it in front of her like a weapon, she tiptoed toward the pantry, careful not to make a sound. If she ripped the door open quickly, she might catch the rodent unawares and be able to smack it right out of the kitchen door with the broom. Strangely enough, the back door was open; Abbie could see into the courtyard. At least that would make it easy to get the rat outside.

She grasped the handle of the pantry door and listened for a moment. There was no sound, no scurrying of little feet. It was now or never. Taking a deep breath, Abbie yanked the door open and leaped into the pantry, and nearly knocked Priscilla's head off with the broom.

"Abbie!" Priscilla yelped, throwing up her hands to defend herself.

"Priscilla?" Abbie lowered the broom. "What are you doing in here?" Her eyes traveled past Priscilla, and met with those of a tall, burly man with broad shoulders and close-cropped brown hair. Horror leaped in Abbie's chest, and she grabbed Priscilla's arm, dragging her out of the pantry. "Stay back," she shrieked, brandishing the broom. "Get out of here. We're closed for business."

"Excuse – " the man began.

"Go!" screamed Abbie, waving the broom wildly. "Or I'll – I'll – I'll knock your block off."

The man held up his hands, and his wide eyes made Abbie realise just how young he was. There was only the faintest sprinkling of stubble along his jaw.

"I have no doubt about that," he said, a note of amusement in his tone, "but I'm not going to hurt anyone." He sidled sideways toward the pantry door. "I'll be going now."

Priscilla shook Abbie's hand off and let out a faint chuckle. "It's all right, Robah," she said. "Abbie's a good egg. You can tell her."

She pulled out a chair and flopped down by the kitchen table, digging a pipe out of her front pocket.

"Robah?" Abbie squinted at him. "Wait… you're Priscilla's son?"

"That's right." Robah relaxed, letting his hands fall to his sides. "I'm sorry if we startled you."

"You sounded in such a hurry coming down the stairs that I thought you were Lady Rose," said Priscilla. "She doesn't like Robah to come around here."

"Why?" asked Abbie suspiciously.

"Oh, not for the reasons you think, girl," said Priscilla. She sighed. "I raised Robah to be everything that I will never be." Her voice cracked a little, and she blew out a breath of smoke, turning her face away.

Robah's eyes filled with pain. "Someday I'll get you out of here, Mama."

Priscilla waved a hand, still not looking at him or at Abbie. "I used to tell Robah to stay away from this place," she said, "but these days I let him come because I don't know if he ever eats otherwise." She shook her head, annoyance replacing the sorrow in her tone. "He's an apprentice at the tailor's down the street, and they hardly feed him and barely pay him a penny. And he won't use his money the way he should. He squirrels it away and doesn't buy enough food."

Robah met Abbie's eyes and gave her an embarrassed smile. Something about it warmed Abbie deep inside, and she found herself returning his smile more quickly than she had meant to.

"I keep telling you, Mama, I'm fine," said Robah.

"No, you're not. Look at you," said Priscilla angrily.

Now that Robah was standing closer, Abbie could see what his mother meant. He had strong shoulders and powerful forearms, likely born from hours spend sewing and slaving over the tailor's work. But there was barely any flesh clinging to his chiseled facial features; his legs were thin, and his waist seemed almost smaller than Abbie's.

Overwhelming instinct filled Abbie's heart, and she couldn't stop herself from moving to the pot on the stove, still containing last night's leftovers. Retrieving a wooden bowl from the cupboard, she spooned some cold beef stew into the bowl.

"Here," she told Robah, holding it out.

If his body hadn't already belied his hunger, his eyes did it now, widening as though Abbie had just offered him a glorious feast. He held out a hand, then hesitated. "Are you sure?" he asked. "I... I don't want to steal."

"You're hungry, and Lady Rose has more than enough." Abbie thrust the bowl into his hands. "Eat."

Robah slowly reached out and took the bowl, his face still transfixed with disbelief. Slowly, he raised his eyes from the food to Abbie's face. When they met hers, they lit up brilliantly, and he smiled in a way that took her breath away.

She wasn't sure why, but just looking into Robah's eyes, Abbie felt as though her heart was swelling right out of her chest.

CHAPTER 6

ABBIE KEPT one eye on the kitchen window as she peeled carrots for that afternoon's salad. It was a beautiful, summery morning, and for once the street looked quaint and pretty despite its tumbledown buildings and disreputable characters lurking on the corners. The handful of homes on this street had little strips of garden in front of them, and one or two of the housewives had managed to coax some flowers into growing, their colours splashes of brilliance against the drab browns and greys of the rest of the street. The sunlight smiled down on the sidewalks, and Abbie had even opened the kitchen window to let in a breath of the warm breeze.

Still, it wasn't the beautiful day Abbie was looking at. She laid aside one peeled carrot for chopping and took another, working the peeler quickly across its surface, then glanced back out of the window. The street was still empty of the one familiar figure for which she was searching, and she felt a brief pang of disappointment.

"You'll cut yourself if you keep on staring out of the window like that," said a familiar voice, and Priscilla walked into the kitchen, her pipe in her hand as usual. "All that staring isn't going to make him come any faster."

Abbie felt her cheeks growing hot. She turned her eyes hastily back to her work, reaching for another carrot. "I don't know what you're talking about," she said.

"Oh, I think you do." Priscilla gave a happy chuckle. She pulled out a chair opposite Abbie and sat down, stretching her legs tiredly out in front of her. "Ever since you first met Robah a few months ago, you two have only had eyes for each other."

Abbie's cheeks grew even warmer; she felt in danger of bursting onto flame. "Robah is kind," she said. "He reminds me of my papa. His voice is so..." She paused, trying not to describe the way it made every cell in her body tingle warmly. "Friendly," she managed. "It's nice to be with someone who is kind. That's all."

"Oh, that's all, is it?" Priscilla gave another of her round, meaty chuckles.

Abbie wanted to plunge her face into a bucket of cold water. Flustered, she shoved the carrot peelings into a bucket and reached for the chopping knife. She couldn't stop herself from stealing another glance out of the window at the empty street.

Priscilla laughed again, but when she spoke, her tone was serious. "It's all right, you know," she said with uncharacteristic gentleness. "Robah's a good boy, and you're – not like the rest of us." She sighed. "I don't blame him for liking you. You're innocent and sweet and kind. Nothing like me."

Again, Priscilla turned her face away, and Abbie felt a pang of compassion. "You've always been kind to me, Priscilla," she said. "You know I appreciate that."

"Oh, Abbie." Priscilla sighed out a cloud of smoke. She studied her for a long moment. "I was like you once, you know. And then... well, I got desperate. And this place happened." She shook her head. "I don't know. I am where I am now. But promise me, Abbie, if you love my son, never end up like me."

Tears glittered suddenly in her eyes. "Don't live like me, if you could even call this life. I don't even know who Robah's father is. Wouldn't know his face if I saw him in the street. Don't let this happen to you."

"I won't," said Abbie quickly. "I don't plan on it."

Priscilla gave a harsh, dry chuckle. "No one ever does, child," she said. "But don't let it suck you in."

"Lady Rose gave me her word. I'm just a housekeeper," said Abbie.

Priscilla shook her head sorrowfully. "She just has to keep it," she said quietly. "You know why Robah saves all his money instead of feeding himself properly, don't you?"

"Yes," said Abbie softly. "He wants to get a tenement and move you out of this place to be with him."

Priscilla nodded. "He's a good boy," she repeated. "You be good to him, Abbie. I hope that when the time comes that he has his own tenement, he will move you there, instead of me."

"Priscilla." Abbie gasped, even though the thought of sharing a tenement with Robah made her veins thrill with pleasure. "Of course, he'll help you."

Priscilla got up, groaning quietly. "Sometimes I wish he would give up on me, as I have," she said.

Before Abbie could say anything more, Priscilla left the kitchen, stumbling out toward her room to get ready for a long night's work. Abbie shuddered, thinking of the hopelessness in the older woman's voice. Sometimes it felt as though the very walls of the brothel seeped pure evil. She felt it in her bones, in the pit of her soul, and it made her want to run screaming from the building. She scrubbed out stains every day, yet the brothel never felt clean. But what choice did she have? She had nowhere else to go.

The chilling thought was still blowing coldly across her heart when she looked out of the window again and finally saw him walking up the street toward the brothel's back door, head high, arms swinging, his usual cheerful smile curving his lips. Robah. Abbie's heart felt filled with golden butterflies. She grabbed the sandwich she had made him from the counter and abandoned her carrots on the kitchen table, then hastened out into the courtyard to meet him at the back gate.

"Good afternoon, Robah," Abbie called out.

Robah's smile captured her heart, drawing it like a magnet. "Hello," he said, his voice still holding that full, warm, round timbre that made goosebumps scatter on her body. She was pleased to see that he was still putting on weight; there was some flesh to his shoulders now, some roundness to his face.

"I've made you a sandwich today," said Abbie. She held it out to him. "It's such a beautiful day, I thought you could eat outside. I'll sit with you. Lady Rose is having her afternoon nap. She won't be awake for an hour at the least."

"In that case, I have a better idea." Robah took the sandwich gratefully, and she saw him shudder a little with relief, as though the thought of his next meal had been worrying him all day. "Why don't we take a little walk together?"

"A walk?" Abbie glanced back at the brothel. She had hardly left it, except to go to the market, in years.

"Just a short way." Robah smiled. "There's a park three blocks away. I think you'd like it."

His smile made her feel lighter, as though the grubby sidewalk had turned into fluffy clouds under her feet. She found herself smiling back at him. "All right," she said. "Let's go."

Robah offered her his arm, and Abbie felt a glorious thrill all the way from her toes to the top of her head as she took it, feeling his warmth through his ragged coat. He set off with a long, easy stride, and Abbie felt a wonderful shock as they stepped out onto the busy sidewalk and she realised she was not afraid. There were, as always, grubby men in rags on the corners, and as always, they glanced at her with hunger in their eyes as she passed; but then their gaze would rest on Robah, and they would look away quickly. Perhaps for the first time in her life, Abbie felt free.

As they walked, Robah was talking about everything he saw; the people, the birds, even the colour of the sky and the shape of the clouds. Abbie barely spoke, but she had no need to speak. She simply listened to Robah and delighted herself in everything he said.

The park was an expected jewel tucked among the ugly businesses and scruffy homes. It was tiny – little more than a few abandoned lots, with some vague effort made to keep the grass trimmed. There was a single, drooping willow tree struggling barely to stay alive, and a tiny, muddy pond where a lonely duck sculled around the surface. There was so much sorrow in it all, and yet it was green and alive, and it pierced Abbie's heart with its beauty.

They sat together on a low-slung branch of the willow tree and watched the duck swimming around, pausing occasionally to dabble in the mud. Robah ate his sandwich in enormous, hungry bites.

Abbie let him eat in peace for a few moments before she spoke. "Do you ever eat at the tailor's?" she asked gently.

Robah paused. "Yes," he said. "They give me supper."

Abbie felt a pang of sorrow for him. Lady Rose was cruel, and the brothel was awful, but she had three meals a day, and she had forgotten what it was to go to bed hungry. But Robah had a single meal each day, barring the weekends, when he would come to the brothel and Abbie would feed him as well as she could.

"I'm sorry," she said.

"It's my choice." Robah smiled at her. "I have to get my mama out of that place."

"I know," said Abbie. She sighed, staring down at the pond. "I miss my family so much."

Robah pulled off a tiny piece of his sandwich and tossed it to the duck. Quacking in delight, the duck gulped it down. Abbie felt a sense of pressure from him, as though there was a question he wanted to ask but didn't.

"I had to leave them behind," said Abbie softly.

Robah looked at her, his eyes questioning. "Your family?"

"Yes. They live by the wharves. Lived." Abbie swallowed, realizing afresh with a little twist of her gut that she didn't know if her family still lived in the same tenement, or if they even still lived at all. "My mama is long gone. My brother has been out to sea for years; but my papa and sister..." She let her words trail off.

"I'm sorry that you're not with them," said Robah.

"I had no choice." Abbie glanced sideways at him. She had never told anyone about the murder, not even Priscilla, whom she trusted the most out of all the ladies in the brothel. But could she tell Robah? The weight of her burden of fear hung on her like lead.

"I'm sorry," Robah repeated. He reached toward her, touched the back of her hand lightly with his fingertips, as though he was a little nervous. His touch thrilled her. "You don't have to talk about it."

"I haven't spoken of them in years," Abbie admitted. "Not since I left." She bit her lip. "I want to talk about it, but I'm afraid that it would put them in danger if it reached the wrong ears."

Robah's eyes locked on hers, deep and limpid. "I wouldn't tell a soul," he said quietly.

Abbie believed him. She felt, then, how much she trusted him, sitting with him here in this abandoned little park, two feet of air still safely between them. Robah had not so much as looked at her the way every other man always did.

She reached for his hand. He took hers as if he had been waiting for it.

"I couldn't stay," she said softly. "I couldn't stay with my family. They would all be in danger."

"I don't understand," said Robah.

"You can't. I can't tell you," said Abbie. "It would only put you in danger..." She felt tears sting her eyes. "I can't put anyone in danger. I'm already in danger myself... I..." She felt her words trail off, panic gripping her. It was replaced steadily by sorrow. "I can never go back," she said. "I can never see my family again because of... him."

Robah squeezed her hand. "He's not going to hurt you," he said. "I'll see to that."

She smiled at his protectiveness, even though she knew he couldn't make good on his promise; the words were a reaction, a knee-jerk in response to her peril. "Thank you, Robah," she said.

He smiled at her. "Your secret's safe with me."

Abbie nodded, but a cold knot of fear and regret was gathering in the pit of her belly. Hopefully, she hadn't revealed too much. She could only hope that he would always be safe.

CHAPTER 7

EVEN THOUGH SHE had to juggle all of the groceries for an entire week in the brothel all the way home, market day was still Abbie's favorite day of the week. It was a chance for her to be no one at all; just a face in the crowd, not someone for men to stare and assess the way she assessed the cuts of meat in the butchery, not someone for the ladies of the night to push around and treat like a slave. She could melt away among the scores of other women who came to the market square for their weekly groceries, and just become a shadow, safe and ignored.

She walked home in the summer sunshine, enjoying the rare warmth, her arms loaded down with baskets and paper bags and parcels tied with string. It was a lovely day, and her thoughts were quick to turn to Robah. She loved the way he looked at her. It completely lacked that harsh, analysing look that most men had; there was no hunger in his eyes, but there was something else, something that burned low and deep. She knew it because she felt it in her own heart every time she laid eyes on him. And his voice… it was so warm, billowing around her like a great, warm blanket.

She closed her eyes, ignoring the discomfort in her arms for the sake of her daydream, and felt a smile tugging at her lips. It had been so long since she had felt she had something more in her life than mere survival. Robah had given her hope.

When she opened her eyes on the street corner, she saw him.

The pale-eyed man. The man with the knife.

The murderer.

Abbie's heart thumped violently in her throat, sweat breaking out on her palms as she looked into his cold, colourless eyes. She felt her stomach constrict, and bile stung the back of her throat. There was a crash and a tinkle as a bottle of cordial tumbled from her fingers; it pooled around her feet, dark as the blood from the man in the alleyway. She could hear him gurgle out his last desperate, ragged breaths…

"Oi. Get out of the way."

Another pedestrian bumped into her, and Abbie stumbled forward a step, still clutching her parcels. The face of the murderer looked up at her from a bench by the post office wall, and she realised that it wasn't him, not really. It was only a woodcut in a newspaper lying on the bench, but astoundingly lifelike. So much so that for an awful moment, Abbie had believed she was face to face with the killer.

Her hands were shaking as she struggled to get all her parcels back under control, knowing Lady Rose would be furious about the cordial. But Lady Rose was a puppy, a mere nothing compared to that pale-eyed man.

She was frozen for a second in trembling indecision, unable to decide whether she should hurry off and forget she ever saw his face, or if she should take the paper. She couldn't read it. Not for the first time in her life, Abbie yearned to be literate, so that she could decipher the meaning of the words surrounding his portrait. They taunted her. They could have said anything; they could have said that he'd been caught, that he'd killed again, that he was searching for her.

She had to find out, even though she was terrified of what could happen should any of the pale-eyed man's associates see her picking up the paper. She glanced around as if she could tell by looking which of the many people surrounding her knew him. Then she snatched it up and stuffed it into a basket with her other parcels and hastened back toward the brothel. It felt as though every shadow reached for her as she moved. As though the pale-eyed man was on her very heels.

༺༻

FOR THE REST of that week, Abbie could think of almost nothing except for the newspaper that lay hidden in the back of the broom cupboard. As she went about her daily tasks in the kitchen, she felt as though the very killer himself were watching her; as though his pale eyes really were looking up from that newspaper, following her every move. He stalked through her dreams, a knife gleaming in each hand. Time and time again, she saw his victims die: the man on the street, her papa, Gail. Robah.

It was Robah that she ended up waiting for. Sometimes, when the pressure of not knowing grew torturous, Abbie considered asking Priscilla to read the paper to her. Priscilla had a little reading, she knew; she'd taught Robah. But Priscilla would ask questions.

As desperately as she needed Robah's help, Abbie regretted telling him even the vague details she'd revealed about her past. Somehow, over the past two years without seeing hide nor hair of the killer, Abbie had started to fear him as a spectre instead of as a real danger. She had begun to hope that chapter of her life was over. Now, the danger felt far too real. Far too close. She couldn't risk endangering any more people because of it.

Robah came at last that following Saturday afternoon, as he always did. Abbie was on her knees in front of the hearth, polishing the grate in small, frantic movements, when she heard that specific little rat-tat on the back door – the knock that Robah always used. Fear and relief washed over her together. The ladies of the night had gone upstairs to prepare for a busy evening; Lady Rose wasn't home. It was just Abbie and Robah on the entire ground floor.

She hurried to her feet, her hands and skirt still smeared with black polish, and pulled the door open with her elbow. She wanted to gasp his name and fall into his arms, but instead, she managed to summon a smile.

"H-hello, Robah," she said.

"Good afternoon." Robah's warm smile settled over her like sunshine, then faltered when he saw her tired, red eyes. "Are you all right?"

"I don't know," Abbie admitted. "Please... come in. Lady Rose isn't here. No one will see you."

Robah's brow was creased with concern as he stepped into the kitchen. Abbie washed her hands quickly at the sink, then reached into the oven, where she'd hidden the plate of food she had saved for him after giving the ladies their lunch. They always had a good lunch on a Saturday: today it was roast chicken, gravy, vegetables, and a mound of mashed potatoes. Robah's eyes grew wide as Abbie took the plate over to the kitchen table and set it down in front of him.

"Please," she said. "Eat."

Robah sank into a chair and stared at the food for a few more seconds, as though he could barely comprehend its existence. Picking up a fork, he took one bite from the mashed potatoes, then look up at Abbie and swallowed.

"Please, tell me what's wrong," he said.

Abbie appreciated the gargantuan effort Robah had made to turn his attention to her instead of the hot meal steaming before him. She sat down opposite him. "All right," she said, "but I'll do it while you eat."

Robah nodded, digging into another bite of potatoes. Abbie took a deep breath, spreading her hands on the table in front of her, as though touching the rough wood could somehow keep her from flying away and being blown to bits in the storm of fear that had assailed her for days.

"I need you to read something for me," she said.

Robah nodded, smiling briefly between bites. "Of course," he said. "What is it?"

"It's... I just... I need to know..." Abbie swallowed hard, trying to control her fear. "I'm not explaining it well. I'll just show you."

She went over to the broom cupboard and retrieved the newspaper from where she had hidden it. Keeping it folded so that the murderer's face was hidden, she brought it to Robah and laid it out on the table. It fell open, and the pale eyes looked up at her from the portrait. She didn't want to see them, but she found herself staring into them, the way a frozen rabbit stares up at the oncoming hawk.

"What is it?" said Robah, picking up the paper, then looking up at Abbie. "I don't understand."

"I need to know who he is," said Abbie.

"This man?" Robah stared at her.

"Yes," Abbie whispered.

She saw him wonder why, but when he read the fear in her eyes, he didn't ask. Instead, he just reached over the table to take her hand. "It's all right," he said. "I'm here."

"What does it say?" said Abbie tearfully. "Please... just tell me who he is. Tell me what he wants."

"I don't understand why you're so afraid," said Robah gently. "This piece in the paper is about some foolish upper-crust society scandal – nothing you need to be worried about. This man is a magistrate's son, a rich man."

"What's his name?" Abbie asked, fearfully, as though hearing the man's name would somehow summon him to her kitchen.

"Hawkins," said Robah. "Leroy Hawkins." He shook his head. "I've heard stories about him. His father dotes on him, and he has anything he wants... and does anything he wants." A visible shudder ran down Robah's spine. He stared at Abbie, comprehension filling his face. "Abbie, when you said that your family was in danger... was it because of this man somehow?"

Abbie's knees felt weak. "I should never have told you about him," she breathed. "You're... you're in... you're in danger."

Her knees buckled, and Robah jumped up from his chair, grabbing her arms. His touch pulled her back from the brink of fainting as he guided her into a chair and crouched in front of her, his hands still steady on her arms, immovable.

"Are you in danger?" he asked softly.

Tears filled Abbie's eyes. She allowed them to roll down her cheeks, fear pressing down on her like the pressure of a coming storm.

"I can't tell you," she sobbed. "I can't tell you anything."

"Please, Abbie," Robah begged. "Just tell me what happened. Tell me who this man is. Maybe I can help you somehow."

"No." The word came out with more force than Abbie had intended. "No," she said, more softly. "I won't. I must keep you safe." She got up quickly, wiping her eyes on the sleeve of her dress. Her voice was a little steadier. At least the article in the paper was just about Leroy Hawkins' scandalous behaviour; there was nothing in it to indicate that he was close by, or somehow more of a threat to her than before, or Robah would have told her.

"Forget I ever asked you about him," said Abbie.

"But I want to protect you," said Robah. "I want to know how I can help you."

She saw the desire, rich and genuine, shining in his eyes, but she knew she could never accept his help. She would rather feel the edge of Leroy Hawkins' knife than see it plunged into Robah.

"Sit and eat, Robah," she said stiffly. "Forget about all of it."

Robah backed away, pain in his eyes. "Don't you trust me?" he said softly.

"I do." Abbie looked away. "I love you."

The words came out unbidden, slipping through her lips before she could stop them, but once they were spoken, she realised how true they were. She stared at Robah for a moment, and his gentle eyes looked back, wide with surprise and mixed emotions.

"You do?" he breathed.

"Always," Abbie whispered. She dropped her eyes to the floor. "And I need you to trust me. Please. Don't ask questions about... that man. Just... forget about him." She took a deep breath, smoothing down her dress, and seized the newspaper from the table. "Finish your meal," she said. "I have work to do."

"Abbie..." Robah began.

Abbie was already striding out of the kitchen. On her way out, she threw the paper into the fire. The flames wrapped around Leroy Hawkins' face and devoured it in a flicker of yellow and gold.

※

Rain draped the city in a grey curtain. Silver streaks of falling droplets covered Abbie's vision; the gutter sang and splashed beside her as she walked along the sidewalk, and sprays of water gushed up from the wheels of the carts that rushed by periodically.

A brewer's dray hurried by too close, and Abbie jumped aside, but she was too late. Filthy water splashed against her skirt, soaking her left leg instantly to the skin. Cold clutched at her, and she pulled her holey coat a little tighter around her shoulders, hoping at least to keep part of her torso dry.

It didn't feel like summer today. The grey light and the hiss of rain made it feel like a dismal autumn day. Then again, every day had been dismal lately, no matter how much the sun might shine. Everything had felt grey and flat and lost since her time with Robah.

He hadn't come by that weekend. Priscilla, in her worry, had eventually sneaked out to take him some food. She had returned with the news that Robah was well but had too much work to get away from the tailor. Abbie knew that couldn't be true. He was angry with her, and he had every right to be. She had kept secrets from him. What was worse, she had divulged part of those secrets to him, and put his very life in danger.

She trudged along the street on her way back to the brothel, trying her best not to let the rain soak into the loaves of bread she carried in her arms. Rain had made its way into her hood, and she could feel it dripping icily down the nape of her neck. It was as cold and unwelcome as the despair brooding in her gut. She should have known not to allow herself to love Robah so much. She should have remembered that because of Leroy Hawkins, she could never have anyone close to her again.

Yet life without the people she loved felt as grey and cold and miserable as the rain.

Abbie had reached the corner of the street. She paused, looking into the traffic, hoping for a break so that she could make her way across. One of the loaves already felt squishy in her arms. Lady Rose would be angry. Lady Rose was always angry.

Then, through the fog of cold and misery that shrouded her soul, Abbie heard it.

Gail's laugh.

Papa had always said that Gail sounded just like Mama when she laughed. Abbie closed her eyes, savouring the sweet, golden memory of her sister. Gail hadn't laughed often, but when she did, it was as though she had stored all the joy and beauty of a thousand ordinary giggles inside the very heart of one perfect sound, and it all came leaping out of her when she laughed. The sound was golden and musical, soft and rhythmic, and it washed over Abbie's tired soul like warm honey.

Of course, Abbie knew it could not be Gail's laugh that she was hearing, not really. Even though her feet unfailingly led her to the marketplace that was nearest to the wharves, Abbie had never dared to actually set foot back in the wharves, not since she had left. It had been torture, sometimes, to know that she could so easily go home. Yet every time the knowledge of the danger that would cause them had stopped her from doing it.

She opened her eyes, still feeling a haze of joy. She must have heard the laugh somewhere in her head, or perhaps some other girl in this crowded marketplace just sounded enough like Gail to jog the memory. Abbie let out a slow sigh. She wondered if she would ever hear Gail's voice again.

She stepped forward again, ready to get back to the brothel. The grocery was right in front of her, and as she walked in its direction, a large cart standing in front of it moved aside.

And Gail was standing there – the real Gail, in the flesh.

Abbie knew her at once. Even though Gail had her back to Abbie, even though she had womanly curves now that had not been there before, Abbie knew it was her sister standing there perusing the fruits and vegetables on display in the grocery window. She was wearing a maid's uniform, pressed and neat, and as Abbie stared, she turned. For a shocking moment, Abbie looked into Gail's face. Her cheeks were red and rosy, and a beautiful smile transfixed her expression.

Everything in Abbie compelled her to run forward, to cast aside her groceries and fling her arms around her sister and never, ever let her go again. Yet before she could take a single step, Abbie was gripped with awful fear. She couldn't go to Gail. In fact, she had to get as far away from Gail as possible, as quickly as she could – before she tainted her with the same curse that had been laid upon Abbie on that awful night in that dark alley.

Tears strangled her, and for a long moment, Abbie feared she would not be able to turn around. Gail's eyes had glanced over her without seeing her; she was looking back at the grocery window now, selecting some fruit. She hadn't noticed. She was happy. She was safe.

The knowledge gave Abbie just enough strength to turn around and run the other way. Somehow, she managed to contain her tears until she had ducked around the street corner. It was only then that she allowed herself to weep wholeheartedly; partially out of relief to see that Gail was all right, and partially out of the awful, appalling reality that she knew she could never hold her sister in her arms again.

CHAPTER 8

ABBIE NOW HAD a small room in the servants' quarters on the second floor, but the only place that really felt like home in the brothel was the kitchen. Customers seldom came down here; even Lady Rose hardly ever deigned to set foot inside the kitchen. It was Abbie's safe place, where everything was laid out exactly the way she liked it, and she was in command of everything from the stock of flour to what the ladies would have for supper.

Supper was long over now, though; the last leftovers had been cleared away, the dishes cleaned and returned to their cabinets, and even the floor was swept and polished. Still, Abbie sat on an uncomfortable wooden chair in front of the hearth, her feet outstretched toward the flames. She didn't want to go up to her room now. It was just too close to the other rooms – the rooms where the business was conducted. She didn't even like to think about the things that the ladies, many of whom had become her friends, were doing.

She gazed into the flames instead, thinking about Papa and Gail. As much as hearing Gail's laugh had felt like a gift, her soul was weary now beneath the weight of her longing. There were times when she could forget how much she missed them. But now, she felt as though her loneliness was strangling her.

She wished Robah would come. Her heart ached. Maybe, on Sunday morning, she could sneak out of the brothel and go to the tailor's. Perhaps he would listen to her if she spoke to him.

Perhaps she should tell him the truth... but the truth would put his life at risk.

The tangle of Abbie's thoughts consumed her, and she felt she was sinking away into total despair. Her mind was so filled with her fears that she didn't notice the kitchen door had opened until she heard the footsteps coming into the room.

Abbie looked up. A tall gentleman in an emerald-green dress coat had just come into the kitchen. He wore canary jodhpurs and long black boots, and there was something about the twirl of his moustache and the gleam in his piercing blue eyes that made Abbie's stomach twist with fear.

She got up, awfully aware of the way his eyes roamed over her, reckless and without respect.

"Excuse me, sir," she said, her voice faint and trembling. "I believe you've made a wrong turn. The rooms are back the way you came." She lifted a finger, pointing.

The man regarded her for a long moment. She had that feeling again that she was nothing but a prize cut of meat in his eyes; a product, to be assessed and rejected or purchased. The corner of his mouth quirked, and he buried his hands in the pockets of his lovely coat, leaning against the doorframe.

"Oh, I don't think I'm lost at all," he said.

His voice was smooth, velvety, educated, and it slithered across Abbie's skin like slime. She glanced toward the back door, her heart thumping in her chest. It was locked, as usual at this time of night. The key was in her pocket. Could she be quick enough?

"Please allow me to show you the way back to the counter, sir," she quavered.

The gentleman straightened up and took a step toward her. Despite the alcohol fumes rolling off his every breath, he moved with a long, low step, easy and slinking. Like a stalking wolf.

"I think I'm right where I need to be," he said, his voice lower and more dangerous with every syllable. "My tastes normally run a little older… but perhaps I'm looking for something young and fresh tonight."

Abbie's heart was thundering in her mouth. She backed away, heading slowly for the back door, and reached into her pocket for the key. "Sir, I'm not…" She hesitated. "I'm not one of the ladies."

"You're in a brothel, girl." The man gave a mirthless laugh. "It's only a matter of time in any case."

Abbie's back bumped against the door. She took a deep breath, steeling herself for her next move: to spin around, unlock it, and bolt for all she was worth. But before she could move, the man was upon her. One hand slamming into the door next to her head, the length of his body thudded against her own, pinning her against the wood. His free hand snatched the key out of hers and threw it across the kitchen. It skidded across the floor, hopelessly out of reach, and

Abbie was trapped, her face mere inches from the gentleman's face.

He let out a breathy, satisfied laugh and leaned closer to her so that his lips brushed her ear when he spoke. "Don't try to fight," he whispered. "Or do, if you want to. Nothing will help."

"No!" Abbie squealed, panic seizing her limbs. She tried to lunge out of his reach, but he seized her by the throat with a swift movement and slammed her back against the door. His fingers were tight around her windpipe; she dragged in a strangled breath and brought up her knee, quick and hard. The man roared and stumbled back, doubling over, and Abbie screamed with all of her might. She bolted, pushing past the man, but he was already recovering. As she fled past him, an arm was thrown around her knees and Abbie fell headlong. Her hands smacked into the kitchen floor just in time to save her face, her knees burning, the breath knocked from her, and the man's hands closed like shackles around her ankles.

"You're a fighter," he snarled, hauling her closer, her fingernails scrabbling desperately on the floor. "But you're going to lose."

"No. Help!" Abbie screamed. "Help!"

The man had switched his grip from her ankles to her knees now, and then he reached higher, gripping the flesh of her thigh with hard fingers, and Abbie's pleas for help turned into a long, wordless shriek as pain and terror filled her world.

The kitchen door slammed open, the sound reverberating through the room. The man froze, and Priscilla came striding through the doorway in a splendour of rage and finery. She wore a flowing red gown that swooped low over her chest and pinched her waist to an impossible proportion. The skirt flowed like fire across the floor around her, and the same fire blazed in her eyes as she shouted, "Let her go."

The man's grip faltered on Abbie's leg. She wrenched it from his grasp, feeling his fingernails rip through her stockings, and scrambled to her feet in a single panicked movement. She rushed to Priscilla's side, and the older woman grabbed her arm and pulled her close. Her face was heavily painted and powdered, but that only served to highlight the rage written upon it.

"Firebird." The man breathed the name Priscilla used for customers in two hot, damp gasps. His hair was in disarray, his face very red, and there was sweat on his brow. "There you are," he purred.

"You've known where I am all this time, Hugh," spat Priscilla. "I've seen you once a week for many years, every time your wife visits her sister, but never did I imagine you would be fool enough to accost an innocent girl."

The man's eyes flashed, his hands balling into fists. "Choose your words carefully, woman," he roared. He strode up to her, his eyes burning. "Remember that I am a lord, and you – you're nothing but an old…" He called Priscilla a name that was not untrue, but that nonetheless made Abbie's skin crawl.

"I am," said Priscilla unflinchingly. "You're right. But this is just an innocent girl. A maidservant. Leave her be." She took a step forward, shoving Abbie behind her, and laid a smooth white hand on Hugh's chest. "You have me. Leave her alone."

Hugh seized Priscilla's hand and shoved her back hard enough that she stumbled on her high heels.

"You've been insubordinate to me, woman," he spat. "You are nothing."

The tap-tap-tap of heeled shoes on the hallway announced the arrival of Lady Rose. Abbie cowered back as Lady Rose swept into the kitchen, imperious and majestic, her greying hair piled high on her head.

"What is the meaning of this?" she cried. "Firebird, how dare you shout at an esteemed customer in that manner?"

Priscilla turned to Lady Rose. Abbie saw a flash of fear in her eyes, then they grew cold, calculating. "I was just wondering what Lord Kinley was doing here in the kitchen, ma'am," she said. "Isn't it strictly off-limits to customers?" An edge crept into her voice.

Lady Rose glanced over at Abbie. Her eyes lingered on Abbie's tear-streaked face, and comprehension dawned in them.

She looked back at Lord Kinley, her voice smooth and calm. "Nothing is off-limits to Lord Kinley, Firebird," she said. "You of all people should know that by now."

Something dark and frightened crossed Priscilla's face.

Lady Rose turned to the enraged man. "I apologize for the absolutely inexcusable behaviour of my employees, sir," she said. "You know you're one of our most valued and regular customers. Tell me how I can make amends. Anything you want."

Lord Kinley's cold eyes were fixed on Priscilla. "I want her gone," he said.

Lady Rose hesitated. "Firebird?" she said.

"Yes. Get rid of her," said Lord Kinley. "I cannot stand the presence of a woman who speaks to me in that manner. I will not be returning to your establishment if I ever see her again. And neither will any of my friends."

Lady Rose swallowed. "Yes, sir," she said quietly.

Priscilla grew as pale as a ghost. Guilt filled Abbie, and she stepped forward. "Please, ma'am, it's not her fault," she begged. "I was the one who screamed. Don't punish her."

She saw the blow coming, but she knew better than to move. Lady Rose slapped her across the face with ringing agony, and Abbie stumbled back.

"It's time you learned to be silent, child," she thundered. She turned to Lord Kinley. "Firebird is dismissed as of this moment. Now, allow me to show you to one of our other ladies. You will find her most satisfactory."

"There's no time for that now," snapped Lord Kinley. "But when I return, I know which one I want as Firebird's replacement." He raised an imperious finger and pointed at Abbie.

Abbie felt ice cold all over. Before she could even console herself with Lady Rose's promise, the older woman broke it.

"She will be ready for you next weekend, sir," she said primly.

"She had better be," growled Lord Kinley.

He swept Abbie once with a glance that ran her through like a knife. Then, shoving Priscilla out of the way, he swept out of the kitchen.

PRISCILLA'S worldly belongings were not quite enough to fill a single cloth drawstring bag. She looked small and deflated to Abbie as she sat at the kitchen table, watching as Abbie packed some stolen food into the bag: a loaf of bread, a few apples, a few slices of cold meat wrapped in brown paper. Some of the other ladies had gathered around in sombre silence.

The only sound was Abbie's quiet sniffling. She tried her best to hold back her tears, but her body and heart were rebelling against her, refusing to be strong for Priscilla. The older woman was sitting very straight and very silent in her chair. Stripped of her makeup and her fine red gown, she was wearing a plain old dress that might once have been pretty, four or five owners ago. Her face looked grey and faded, but all of its lines were still and stern. She had cried no tears.

Abbie closed the bag and pushed it across the table to Priscilla. The movement seemed to jolt the older woman out of her reverie, and she looked up at Abbie, creasing her face into some semblance of a smile.

"Thank you, dear," she said, taking the bag. "I appreciate it."

"Priscilla..." Abbie swallowed her tears with an effort. "I'm so sorry."

"No." Priscilla's voice was low and firm. She reached across the table and gripped Abbie's hand in a trembling, iron claw. "Don't be sorry. Not for anything. I'm glad I chased that monster off you." Her eyes relented. "Now at least you have time to prepare for what's going to happen."

Abbie felt sick at the thought of what lay in store for her that weekend. She pushed the thought aside. "But what will you do?" she said. "Where will you go?"

"I don't know," Priscilla admitted. "But don't worry, dear. I'll find a way." She sighed, looking out of the window at the bright summer sky. "I always have."

Abbie thought of Robah, and her heart felt like it was being slowly crushed. "When you see Robah..." She hesitated. "Tell him I'm sorry... and that I miss him."

"I'll tell him, darling," said Priscilla. She squeezed Abbie's hand. "And I'll tell him to come and see you. He shouldn't miss out on such a good girl."

Abbie felt a tear rush down her cheek. "Don't," she said. "I won't be a good thing anymore soon." She choked on her tears. "Priscilla, I don't know what to do."

"You'll be all right, Abbie," said Daisy, interjecting herself into the conversation. "It's not so bad. It makes you hard. Besides, you'll make good money, even if Lady Rose takes the lion's share."

"Yes, you'll see," said Sally. Her eyes were still hollow, but she managed a smile. "You'll become a sister to us, and we'll take care of you."

There were a few moments of silence, and then Priscilla stood up, taking the drawstring bag. She slung it over her shoulder and turned to Abbie.

"Don't listen to them," she said. "They're trying to make themselves feel better, just like I did. They're telling themselves the lies I told myself and Sally and all the rest of them. It's not all right. You don't get used to it. Every time – it feels like a piece of your soul is crumbling away." She grabbed Abbie's shoulders in both hands and stared down into her eyes. "Don't let it take you, Abbie. Don't do it. You'll become a shell like me, hollow on the inside, and you're better than that. You deserve better than that." Her eyes were burning. "Fight. Run. Do whatever you have to do to get away."

Before Abbie could respond, Priscilla had turned on her heel and pushed open the back door. She walked away with her head held very high, and her shoulders very upright. And the deafening silence in the kitchen confirmed every word she had said.

But Abbie didn't know if she had the strength to face either fate.

CHAPTER 9

THE METAL SPOON rattled against the sides of the pot as Abbie stirred, making a sound that seemed to echo throughout the brothel regardless of the voices that filled the building as they did every Friday night. She tried to stop her hand from shaking, but it felt impossible. Everything inside her was shaking; her heart felt like it might jump clean out of her chest.

She had been so much more confident of her plan yesterday. Priscilla's words had spurred her on, and she had been working on it all week, ironing out the little details, running through it a thousand times in her mind. Even though escaping on a Friday night felt like cutting it much too close when Lord Kinley was due back on Saturday, Abbie knew that the busier it was, the easier it would be to slip out of the back door unnoticed. Lady Rose had been watching her like a hawk lately, as if she knew that Abbie would try to run.

But surely Lady Rose wouldn't be watching her tonight, not while she was busy waiting on her customers. It was her only chance. Her plan had to work.

She paused in stirring the broth and scooped out a spoonful to taste out of sheer habit. This would be her last act of love to the ladies here; their habits appalled her, but they had been kind, as well as they could. The broth would boil quietly all night, and at least they'd be guaranteed a hot meal tomorrow.

Abbie glanced up at the clock on the kitchen wall, and nervousness shot through her. It was a quarter to eight. She would flee at ten minutes past eleven. The public house down the street closed at eleven sharp, and drunken revellers, not done with a night of carousing, would flood into the brothel. No one would notice her then.

She had felt no shame about stealing from Lady Rose. A full bag of food was sitting by the back door, hidden underneath some potato sacks. Priscilla had mentioned the name of the tailor where Robah worked. She would go there to say goodbye. She had no doubt that Robah no longer wanted her, or he would have come for her by now if his mother had told him what had happened. But she had to see him one last time to say goodbye.

"Abbie."

Abbie jumped. The spoon rang noisily against the side of the pot, and scalding broth splashed onto her hands. She spun around as Lady Rose's voice shrieked her name again.

"Abbie. Come here."

Her heart pounded in all the wrong places. Lady Rose should be busy with customers. What did she want? Had Lord Kinley come early? Maybe she should take the bag and run. But Lady Rose would pursue her at once. Would she stand any chance of escape?

"Abbie." Lady Rose strode into the kitchen. "I'm calling you."

"I'm s-sorry, ma'am." Abbie swallowed. "I... ah... I didn't hear you."

Lady Rose glared at her for a tense moment. Then she shook her head. "Come with me," she barked.

She turned on her heel and stalked off down the hall, and Abbie scurried after her, her heart in her mouth. She dared not ask where they were going, nor did she dare to disobey. She couldn't afford to make Lady Rose suspicious.

Instead, it was suspicion that rose in Abbie's own heart as Lady Rose led her toward the back rooms, the ones where the ladies of the night were conducting their awful business. Abbie's heart beat harder and harder, but there was no time to flee.

She felt a brief moment's relief as Lady Rose turned abruptly and took her into one of the dressing rooms. Perhaps one of the ladies had a torn dress and simply needed a last-minute patch. The room was familiar to Abbie; it was plain and sparse, in sharp contrast with the opulence of the other rooms, and only Daisy was still sitting at the dressing table, applying the last of her makeup.

"Get her dressed," Lady Rose ordered.

Abbie glanced at Daisy, surprised; she was already wearing her usual pink dress. Daisy got up and turned to Abbie. "What do you want me to dress her in?" she asked.

Awful terror shot through Abbie's body. "What?" she gasped.

"She'll fit Priscilla's Firebird dress. Make it quick," said Lady Rose, and swept out of the room.

The door slammed shut behind her, leaving Abbie staring right into the face of her worst nightmare. Her heart was hammering now, her limbs burning with shock, and nausea clutched at her stomach. Daisy had already taken Priscilla's red dress down from the rack and was approaching Abbie with it.

"Don't look so frightened, girl," she said. "You'll be all right."

"I have to go." Abbie started backing toward the door. "I have to get out of here. I'm not going to do this. I can't. I won't!"

She turned and bolted for the door, but the moment she yanked it open, Lady Rose was standing in the entrance. The older woman seized Abbie by the hair and jerked her head back with searing pain.

"You will stop your fuss at once," barked Lady Rose. "No amount of fighting will save you."

"Let me go!" Abbie shrieked, grasping at Lady Rose's hand.

Lady Rose shook her. The movement made her teeth rattle, snapping shut on the inside of her cheek. Blood filled her mouth, tasting like metal.

"A new and most esteemed customer is here," she said, her voice smooth and cold. "He wants a younger girl. He'll get one, and fighting is useless. No one denies Leroy Hawkins what he wants."

Leroy Hawkins. The name shot through Abbie's veins like ice. She felt the world spin around her, her eyesight growing dim. She felt her limbs wobble, and Lady Rose released her grip on her hair. Abbie stumbled backwards, only barely keeping her feet.

"Now get dressed," said Lady Rose icily. "And make it quick. Mr. Hawkins is waiting."

Abbie felt as though she had been suspended in ice water. She couldn't have moved even if she had wanted to; and the terror surging through her mind seemed to have made her thoughts congeal. They barely moved through her mind at all. She was only vaguely aware of Daisy pulling her plain dress off, yanking Priscilla's red dress over her head, lacing it up quickly in the back. It was so strange to feel the cold air on so much of her chest. She did not resist. She could not have resisted any more than a wooden puppet could have; Abbie's heart had frozen in her chest.

She was barely conscious of Lady Rose coming back into the room, grasping her arm and leading her out into the hallway. Her memories were far more real and vivid to her: the quick slash of the knife, the gush of blood, the dying man's gurgle. That was about to become her reality. She knew it.

She knew it even before Lady Rose opened the parlour door, switching her grip on Abbie's hair to her hand, and led her inside with a smooth smile. "A younger girl, Mr. Hawkins," she said. "Just as you wished."

There was a man standing by the fireplace with his back to them when they came in, and when he turned, Abbie felt the blood draining from her face.

His pale eyes were utterly unchanged. They locked on hers, and she saw a flicker within them as he remembered her.

The silence stretched between them, tight as a bowstring. Abbie realised she was shaking uncontrollably. Lady Rose was still smiling, but she gave Abbie's hand a crushing squeeze, mashing the small bones together. Telling her to stop trembling, no doubt, but Abbie may as well have been a dry leaf in a winter gale.

When the silence had gone several seconds past intolerable, Lady Rose spoke. "I trust she will be to your satisfaction, sir?"

Hawkins' smile curved like the edge of a scythe. "Oh, yes," he said, his voice low and dark as a bloodstain on the street. "She'll be quite satisfactory, I'm sure."

"Excellent." Lady Rose smiled and held up Abbie's hand.

Hawkins was coming closer. His predatory smile never left Abbie's face; she felt helpless, a baby hare crouching on barren earth with the circling hawk just above. He took Abbie's hand from Lady Rose's, and his hand was smooth as a baby's, except that Abbie knew it was the same hand that had taken a human life as she watched.

"Yes," Hawkins murmured. His breath against her face smelled of cigar smoke. "You'll do nicely."

"Room number six is open for you, sir," said Lady Rose. She curtsied and withdrew.

The moment Lady Rose was gone, Hawkins' eyes changed. A terrible playfulness came into them, the expression of a cat about to start toying with some small and helpless prey animal.

"Room number six it is, then," he said. He leaned a little closer, whispered the next words into her ear, so close that his lips brushed her skin and made a thrill of awful horror run through her body. "Pretty lady."

Abbie would have gulped for breath, if she had had the strength to breathe at all. Instead, she found herself stumbling along after him as he led her up to room number six. She hated that room, hated every time she cleaned its corners and did its laundry; it was decorated in a vile vomit green, contrasting with fuchsia bedclothes. It looked ridiculous, a parody of a real bedroom. She had never seen it before at night. With only low red lights burning inside the room, it looked like some dungeon of suffering.

Hawkins had been leading her by the hand as gently as if she was made of china, but when he slammed the door behind them and turned to face her, the red lighting etched black shadows across his face, giving him the eyes of a demon.

"I know you know me," he growled, his upper lip curling to reveal a flash of white teeth. "I knew it the moment you laid eyes on me."

Abbie's heart thumped in her chest as if it might break the bars of her ribs and flee. She stared into his eyes. There was no fear in them, but there was danger, and hunger, and that awful lightness, as though confronting the girl who had witnessed a murder he had committed was nothing but a joke to him. As though she was nothing but an object, a toy to play with and discard, no threat at all.

Maybe that was her only hope. Maybe she could be an object: something dead and flat, with no memories, no thoughts.

"Know you?" she said, dropping her voice an octave, trying in vain to grasp that same low tone that Priscilla used on her customers. "I'm sure I soon will, sir."

Hawkins' smile widened. "Sly little vixen," he said. "Are you trying to fool me?" He took a step closer to her, closed his hands possessively around her waist, yanked her up against him. "Don't worry," he whispered. "I won't kill you right away. I'll have my way with you first."

Abbie's eyes slid sideways to the open window. A summer breeze filtered through it, and the street lamps sparkled down below. It could be either death or escape to her. She didn't care which; either would be better than the darkness in Hawkins' eyes.

"That's what you're paying me for," she said, taking a step back, as if she was moving toward the bed. He followed her, not realizing that she was heading for the window. His eyes searched hers. "I couldn't have known, two years ago, that you'd turn out so lovely," he said. "It seems almost a shame now, that you remember."

"Remember what, sir?" asked Abbie. Another step back. The window was almost within reach.

Hawkins gave her a long, calculating look. "You must have seen," he said. "I saw your face. I caught you afterwards. Unless..." He paused. "Maybe you peasants really are so dull and witless that you don't remember."

"That must be the case," said Abbie.

She leaned a little closer to him and felt his breath hitch, but she was so close, so close, and as she reached around him, her fingers closed around the gas lamp on the nightstand. She took a quick breath and moved with all the strength she could muster, bringing her arm up and in. The lamp smacked loudly against the back of Hawkins' head.

He bellowed like an angry bull, lunging at her. His fingernails clawed across her low bodice, but he was dazed from the blow, and she slipped between his fingers and bolted for the window.

"Stop. STOP!" roared Hawkins. "Come back here, you foul heifer."

Abbie's hands slammed against the windowpane, sending cracks across its surface, tiny shards of glass pricking into her skin. It swung open, and Abbie didn't hesitate. She felt

Hawkins' hand brush her leg as he grabbed at her dress, and she flung herself through the open window without thinking twice.

For an awful moment, her dress tightened around her waist, and she realised that he had her. But the dress was old, and she had mended it often. There was a long, ripping sound, and Abbie fell. She had just enough time to throw her arms up over her head before she landed heavily on the canvas roof of a dog-cart parked at the back of the building. It ripped around her, wooden reinforcing snapping and slashing across her skin, and she landed on the back seat with a thump that knocked the air from her.

There was shouting in the brothel; there was shouting in the street. Abbie felt warm blood trickling across her skin, and her mouth was filled with blood. She struggled for vain sips of air, her toiling chest burning with agony, and stumbled out of the dog-cart.

"Don't let her get away!" shrieked Hawkins.

Abbie was hurt, but she knew she was alive, and she also knew that if Hawkins caught up to her, he wouldn't let her get away again. She had to flee. She had to escape and get as far away from this place as she possibly could.

Once again, she felt the wrench of her life being torn away from her. But she had no choice. Limping, gasping, her dress torn, her skin bloodied, Abbie stumbled off into the unknown.

PART III

CHAPTER 10

Two Years Later

It was raining, but then again, it was almost always raining. Abbie had never realised just how seldom London had any sunshine in the spring, not until she had first started living on the streets two years ago, when she had barely managed to escape from the brothel with her life.

The rain hissed and splattered on her bonnet, soaking her quickly through to the scalp. She could feel her dripping hair tickling the back of her neck; it had been so long once, but she had had to cut it off two winters ago, when lice had infested her head. Now it tickled her, adding to the list of realities that were goading her mercilessly as she walked down the crowded street.

It had been two days since her last meal and her arms and legs felt as though they were composed of wet bread instead of muscle. They ached, wobbling with each step, and Abbie had to fight to keep her limbs moving.

If only somehow the hearts of the rich – or even of the moderately middle-class – could be softened. Abbie had spent the entire morning on the corner of a marketplace while housekeepers and housewives bustled to and fro from one stall to the other. The stalls were all groaning with delicious food, juicy orange carrots, great red apples, long cuts of meat, fat yellow cheeses. Abbie would have been delighted by the very scraps of those things, and all the shoppers went home with full baskets. Yet no matter how she clasped her hands and widened her eyes and pitched her voice as high as she could to seem younger than her eighteen years, begging was absolutely unsuccessful. She was lucky to be ignored; kicks and curse words were more commonly her lot. She had earned far more of those than pennies this morning.

In fact, she had but one penny, the tiny shape hard and round at her fingertips as she kept her hands buried in the pockets of her sodden dress. Today would be another hungry day. But she couldn't have stayed out there for a moment longer; already, she was soaked to the skin, and it felt as though the cold was crawling right down into the marrow of her very bones.

She had hoped that taking this new route back to her shelter would have yielded pity from the hearts of passers-by, but it seemed that Londoners everywhere couldn't care less about the ragged figure of some inconsequential street girl. The street she was walking down was a beautiful one; there were warm, well-lit businesses on either side, with brass lettering on the windows and bright wares proudly displayed behind the glass. The men and women hurrying from the businesses to waiting cabs or carriages all wore warm clothes and waterproof shoes. But when she stretched out her hands to the nearest young gentleman, saying, "Alms, sir?" he looked at her as though she was a slug he had just stood upon.

"Get away," he snapped, waving an angry hand at her. "You don't belong here."

Abbie watched the cab drive off, standing briefly in the shelter of a millinery's overhang. The cab splashed off into the rain, and the rest of the world went on sliding past her, muffled and grey. No one even spared her a second glance.

Her eyes skimmed listlessly across the shops opposite and caught a sight that made something jump inside her: men's suits, hanging neatly in a shop window. The tailor was a few shops down across the street from her. She could see the tailor now, showing off bolts of fabric to a young man standing in front of a mirror, his movements quick and servile.

Cold and hunger had lost their edge for Abbie, but there was one thing to which her heart never became impervious, and it was loneliness. It felt like a cancer that had taken root in her heart, and was spreading through her every cell now, making even her bones crumble. Tears stung her eyes. It had been so long since she had had a real conversation with someone.

She missed Robah with every beat of her heart.

Two years had dragged themselves by without him, without anyone. For a long time, she had moved around the city constantly, desperate to avoid the far-seeing pale eyes of Leroy Hawkins and to keep from putting anyone else in danger. But she was growing so tired of running. She was growing so tired of hiding and scrambling to find shelter wherever she could find it. Tired of being chased away from even the filthiest hovels.

And she was only about an hour's walk from the brothel now. She had never returned to that neighbourhood, and she knew she never would... but somehow her feet were carrying her toward the tailor. She knew she shouldn't. She knew she should walk away and keep on running as she had been doing for two years, that the hope growing in her heart was a foolish one, that this would be fruitless just like it had been fruitless every time this spring that she'd walked up to a tailor.

And still, she couldn't stop herself.

She had walked into many tailors in the past few weeks, and she'd learned not to use the front entrance, not in her raggedy state. Instead, she walked around to the back door and pounded on it.

It swung open to reveal a weedy-looking young man with enormous, round eyeglasses. Abbie's heart sank a little. If this was the tailor's assistant, then coming here was already futile.

"What do you want?" demanded the young man, glaring at her.

"Are you the only assistant here?" she asked.

He drew himself up a little. "Yes," he said. "What do you want?"

Abbie turned and walked away, tears filling her eyes. She didn't know why she was so disappointed. After all, Robah might still be apprenticed to the tailor down the road from the brothel, even though she doubted he'd stayed on after Priscilla was cast out. He may have gone looking for somewhere else to work, somewhere that his mother could stay with him, not on the same street as she'd served as a lady of the night for so many years. How many tailors were there in London? A hundred? A thousand?

Would she ever find Robah? Would he welcome the sight of her?

She pressed the heels of her hands against her temples, her sodden hair poking between her fingers. Tears and raindrops ran quietly down her face.

It would be a good thing if she never found Robah. It would keep him safe.

Because Abbie knew that if she ever laid eyes on Robah again, this time, she wouldn't be able to stop herself from telling him everything – including how much she still loved him.

※

ABBIE'S CHEST burned when she woke the next morning, her mind still swirling with dreams.

She had dreamed of Papa and Gail. She'd been dreaming of them more and more regularly over the past few weeks, as her travels through London kept bringing her closer and closer to the wharves before she realised the danger and reluctantly moved away again. Now, she was lying in her makeshift shelter in a back alley out of the wind. It was a pitiful thing – just a few planks and bits of rag spread over a frame of broken boxes – but at least it kept the worst of the rain off her.

Abbie gazed into the drizzle. It felt like it had been raining forever, and a puddle was forming in the middle of the alley. At least it was still a few feet away from the edge of the thin blanket that Abbie slept on.

She had dreamed of Gail's laughter. Papa had been telling them a story as they crowded around the fire in their tenement, his eyes alight with excitement as he told them a fantastical tale about sea serpents and wild storms and exotic countries. Abbie couldn't remember the tale itself now, but she remembered his eyes. They had been as clear as if her dream was a memory.

She closed her eyes tightly, squeezing back her tears. She missed them so much.

Her loneliness and longing grew too heavy for her to breathe. She had to move, to do something to distract herself from it – and besides, the cold had seeped right into her bones. She could die if she just lay here, and when she sat up, the burning in her chest asserted itself, gripping her lungs and making her cough uncontrollably. When the coughing was over, she felt shaky and weak. Her lungs were on fire.

Sally from the brothel, her mother had died of consumption. Abbie wondered if this was what it felt like, and she found herself once again contemplating the possibility of her own death. It was a reality that she had faced so many times over the past two years, but it had still never lost its terrible edge. Fear drove her to her feet, and she stumbled out into the driving rain.

Begging wouldn't work today. She was too old for begging; children were better at it. Besides, something about the rain always tightened people's purse-strings, as though pausing in the wet for the few seconds it took to flip a penny to some poor beggar was just too much effort for most of the rich.

Abbie felt a knot gathering in her stomach as she dragged herself through the streets. Today, she wouldn't be heading into the nice neighbourhood with the tailors and the milliners. She was going deeper into the slum. There were fewer policemen here.

A few minutes later, Abbie had tried to blend in with the crowd that was milling through a marketplace that smelled profoundly of fish oil. She had been to the Billingsgate fish market once; there, well-dressed housewives and housekeepers had haggled over the prices of whole trout, fresh salmon, and live lobsters. This was a very different place. Abbie's holey shoes squelched in mud as she gazed listlessly from one stall to the next. Here, they sold fish heads, and tiny haddock, and suspicious, slimy cuts of greenish-white meat.

It was the old man crouched miserably in a corner, trying in vain to breathe life into a dying fire under a cast iron pot, that caught Abbie's eye. He was prodding bits of damp coal into the smouldering fire; the flames wouldn't rise, and the pot barely steamed at all. The contents were watery and nondescript, but it was food.

Abbie looked at the old man's gnarled hands and paused. For a moment, she considered returning to the alleyway. Perhaps she could sleep through this day and try her hand at begging tomorrow.

But the steady burn in her throat and lungs pushed her forward. She hated the thought of what she had to do, but her alternative was death, a spectre that had been on her heels for so many years that escaping it had become her life's work.

A young man in rags approached the old man with the fish soup. He held out a farthing, and the old man rose stiffly to his feet, scooping some of the watery soup into a wooden bowl. Taking the farthing, the old man held out the bowl.

That was Abbie's chance. She rushed forward, her hands outstretched. There was a yelp of alarm from the old man, but it was already too late. Her fingers closed on the bowl, and she snatched it out of his grip, soup spilling across her hands. There was a gap in the crowd ahead of her, and she plunged forward, on the brink of escape –

A firm hand closed on the back of her dress, yanking her backwards. Abbie landed heavily on her backside; the bowl of soup flew through the air and landed on her lap, splattering her liberally.

"Thief!" bellowed the young man, his skinny hands bunching into fists. He drew one of them back, ready to deal her a terrible blow.

Abbie dodged it just in time. The old man was reaching for her, his hands bent like talons, but she managed to slip out of his grasp. Half crawling, half running, she found her way to her feet. The bowl rolled off her lap and spun away empty, and Abbie slipped into the crowd.

CHAPTER 11

THERE WAS blood on Abbie's hand. It trickled down her fingertips, tracing all of the creases and wrinkles in her skin, and there was a dull, burning sensation across her palm. The sleeve of her dress was soaked.

Abbie's eyes were blinded by tears as she made her way back toward her shelter. She would have to look at her hand as soon as she was out of the rain; she must have landed on something sharp when that young man had pulled her off her feet. She couldn't find it in herself to be angry with him. She had been stealing, after all.

Papa would have been so ashamed. Tears ran down her cheeks, as hot as the blood. She was a disgrace. And worst of all, she was still so, so hungry.

Her hunger would have to wait. Her legs felt too tired to carry her any further; she needed to curl up in her shelter and just rest for a little while. Maybe once she was dry and had slept a little, she would be able to think of a solution.

Another hopeless attack of coughing seized her, and she had to pause on the street corner outside the alleyway, bent double as she coughed and hacked into her elbow. When she drew her arm away, she was half surprised not to see blood on her dress. It felt like her lungs were being burned from the inside out.

She had to get out of the rain. Shivering, she stumbled forward.

She heard the voices right before she could step into the alley. They were a familiar sound to her: coarse, male voices, slurred with alcohol. She had heard them so many times back in the brothel. Fear struck deep into Abbie's stomach, and she slowed, one hand on the wall to support her, as she approached the alley.

Heart pounding, she peered around the corner, and looked straight into the flames that were consuming the only home she had left.

Five young men, one of them swinging a black bottle in one hand, were gathered around the bonfire they had made in the middle of the alley. The alley wall provided some shelter from the driving rain, and the fire leaped high, hot and merry, fuelled by the remnants of Abbie's shelter. She could see the familiar shapes of the planks that she'd used to make the roof; she had so often lain on her blanket and looked up at the stars through the gaps between them. Now, flames were licking around them, turning their edges from black to crumbling grey to nothing.

Her shelter was gone. It had been home and survival to her, but to these young men, it was nothing.

She turned away, pressed her back against the wall and slid to the ground, clutching her wounded hand to her chest. Sobs bubbled up from deep inside her, but her aching body could only sustain the effort of one or two. After that, the tears flowed silently, and Abbie leaned her head back against the wall, her entire being consumed with pain.

She had nothing left not, not even those few scraps of rags and wood that had sheltered her from the bitter rain. It was pouring onto her face now, and she could feel every breath bubble in her lungs; she was not cold, and she knew that that was more dangerous than the shivers that had assailed her earlier. She was sick. And out here in the rain, she could have only one fate.

Perhaps it wouldn't be so bad to just sit here and let her destiny take whatever turns it would. To sit here in the rain and let the darkness take her...

No. The thought sent a terrible jolt of fear through Abbie's body, driving her to sit up, to open her eyes. She had spent so many years fleeing from death at the hands of Leroy Hawkins, yet death had never been closer than it was right now. And now that she was face to face with the spectre, it frightened her more than ever.

A cool breeze rushed against her skin, sending a spatter of rain against her bare cheek. It brought with it a familiar scent: salt and tar, fish and caulking. The smell of the wharves.

Abbie knew she should turn and walk the other way, for her family's sake. But her thoughts dripped slowly through her fevered mind, and she was alone and lost and hungry and desperate and sick, and she knew she would be dead before long. She would face it if she had to, but this was one thing she could not bring herself to face alone.

She turned her feet toward the wharves and stumbled in the one direction she had yearned to take for four long years:

Home.

Trying to find her family was a fool's errand. Abbie told herself this again and again, but her toiling body somehow still found the strength to stumble onward even though every step sapped more strength than Abbie knew she had. It had been four years. They might have moved. They might have died. They might have forgotten her, and even if they didn't, they might never forgive her for what she had done. Abbie could not decide which was more inexcusable: leaving them without an explanation, or returning, placing their lives in jeopardy.

But she could no longer face the city alone. She needed them, even if it was only to see them for the last time, to breathe her love and regret in her last gasp and leave the cruel world behind for greener pastures.

The front door of the tenement still had a missing plank in the bottom. The wind still howled through it, cold and frail as a mourning widow, when Abbie reached it. She could feel her limbs trembling with weakness as she pulled the door open and stumbled up the long stairs.

It felt like too much to hope for that her family would still be there, even though she had retraced her steps all this way. But she had to try. She had to see them one last time. So she paused outside the door to what had once been her home, and she listened.

A sound came from within. A sound that made her heart turn cartwheels, and her very soul bloom like the earth in spring.

Gail. She was singing quietly, the way one sings while working. She had always been absolutely tone deaf, and Abbie would never have recognized the song if it hadn't been one that they had sung together, atrociously badly, so often when they were cleaning the home or selling broth or posies on the corners of the street.

"And did the Countenance Divine shine forth upon our clouded hills?" Gail warbled tunelessly. "And was Jerusalem builded here, among these dark satanic mills?"

Abbie pushed the door open as her sister reached the third line. Gail had her back to Abbie, and she was crouched by the hearth, tucking a few foil-wrapped potatoes into the coals. In a vague blur, Abbie realised that there was a table in the tenement and that the windowpane had been mended. But most of all, she saw her sister; a grown woman now, her plain dress hugging new curves.

"Bring me my bow of burning gold," Gail sang.

Abbie scraped her voice together, choking out a sound between the tears and the pain, to join in the final stanza.

"I will not cease from mental fight, nor shall my sword sleep in my hand, till we have built Jerusalem in England's green and pleasant land."

Gail looked up, blanching ashen white. Her eyes found Abbie's face, and the potatoes fell from her fingers and rolled noisily across the floor.

"Abbie?" she whispered.

Abbie wanted to run to her, to throw herself into her sister's arms. But she only made it one step forward. The world tilted under her feet, and she had just enough time to hear Gail call her name before everything went dark.

CHAPTER 12

It was Papa's voice that jogged Abbie from her deep, fevered sleep. She could not quite make out the words through the fog of her illness, but she could feel his presence, hear the deep burr of his voice close by. Her body felt as though it was floating upon a sea of pain, or perhaps drowning in it, but the sound of his voice soothed her soul. It had been so long, yet she knew it at once.

Startling cold dragged her further from her sleep. There was something icy against her brow; it was uncomfortable, but she didn't have the strength to stir. Words filtered into her exhausted mind. Papa's words.

"... did she come from?" he gasped.

"I don't know, Papa," said Gail. "She just came in here looking like this. I was singing, and I heard her little voice..." Gail sounded choked with tears. "I looked up, and she was standing in the door. And then she just fell."

"Oh, Abbie." Papa's voice was filled with pain and sorrow, as Abbie had been expecting, but there was something more in it, something that made her heart leap with hope. He spoke her name with overwhelming love. "Where have you been, my child?" he whispered, and she felt his big, warm hand stroking her hair.

She had to wake up for him. Forcing her eyelids open, she stared at the ceiling, struggling to clear her blurring vision. "Papa?" she croaked.

"Abbie." Papa's dear face was looking down at her then, a great smile transfixing his weather-beaten features. "Oh, you poor mite."

"I'm so sorry, Papa," Abbie whispered, tears filling her eyes. "I've..."

"Hush. Whatever it is, it doesn't matter." Papa bent down and kissed her forehead, and his cheap-tobacco, fish-oil smell surrounded her like the walls of her home. "Rest now, child. Just rest. Gail and I will care for you."

"We're so glad you're back, Abbie," said Gail.

"No matter what," Papa added.

The thought brought her peace. She floated away slowly, her breaths growing slow and deep, Gail's hand holding hers, Papa's warm touch on her forehead. And if these were her last moments, they were everything that she had wanted.

⚜

THEY WERE NOT her last moments, as it turned out. Abbie woke days later, emaciated, starving, but surviving, thanks to Papa's constant ministrations. It was he who had never left her side during her long coma of fever dreams. Whenever she woke, usually only for brief moments, he was there to coax her to drink some soup, some milk, a little warm tea. He stroked her hair and kissed her cheeks, and when Abbie woke, she was wearing a clean dress. Her hair had been washed and brushed for the first time in years, and she felt human again.

It was nearly a week before she was finally well enough to sit up in bed – a real bed. It was not very large, and the mattress was thin enough that she could feel the bumps of each plank making up the bottom, but it was a bed. She even had pillows, and she leaned against them as Papa sat beside her, stroking her hand.

Gail was at work. Papa had told Abbie that Gail's work was the reason for their comparative prosperity; they could afford food twice a day now, and some meagre sticks of furniture, and to repair the tenement that their landlord refused to maintain. Abbie sipped some sweet, milky tea while Papa told her about it.

"I wouldn't let her go out onto the streets alone without you," he was saying. "I refused to let her sell posies and broth like she always did. So we began to look for work together. She helped me with the fish, and we'd stop by people's homes and businesses, looking for work. That was how she was hired as a kitchen maid."

Abbie remembered seeing Gail that one time near the brothel, wearing a maid's uniform. Her eyes filled with tears as she remembered the appalling wrench it had been to turn her back and walk away.

"Soon after that, she was made a lady's maid to one of the girls in the manor house," said Papa. "She accompanied her to a millinery for measurements, and the milliner offered her work." He smiled. "She's an assistant there now, and she's doing so well. She loves the work, too."

"I'm not surprised," Abbie rasped, her voice still sounding strange and hoarse. "Gail always liked pretty things."

"She wants to be a milliner someday," said Papa. "Perhaps it's a foolish dream, but I'm so proud of her."

"She's grown so beautiful," said Abbie.

"She's grown so *much*." Papa sighed, his eyes growing misty and troubled. "She had to, once you were... gone."

Abbie's eyes stung with tears. She was faced with an appalling dilemma; she was here with Gail and Papa now, and she was alive, which she had not expected. Now what was she going to tell them? How could she keep them safe, and yet abstain from breaking their hearts again by leaving them?

"Oh, Abbie, don't cry." Papa sat down on the bed beside her, wrapping an arm around her shoulders. "Please, darling, just tell me what happened. There is nothing for which I cannot forgive you. Nothing matters. You're safe with me now. Please, just tell me what happened."

"I can't," Abbie sobbed. "I can't."

"Please, Abbie." Papa drew back, wrapping his hands around hers where they still clutched her mug of tea. His eyes were twin pools of pain. "I have to know what it is that I did to drive you away."

"No!" Abbie gasped. "No, Papa, it's nothing like that. I... I just... I can't tell you. It's not safe."

"My dear child." Papa leaned forward, kissed her forehead. "I faced mighty storms on the open sea. Waves as big as mountains, that towered over our ship. I'm not afraid of danger." He squeezed her hands. "Whatever it is, I can protect you."

She wanted to believe him. She had to believe him. She did not have the strength to doubt his words, to hold back her secret any longer.

"I saw a man killed, Papa," she said. "A few days before I left. I saw a... a gentleman cut the throat of a man on the street, and he saw me. He knew I'd seen. He chased after me." She swallowed tears of terror. "He threatened to do awful things to you and to Gail."

"Oh, Abbie." Papa's eyes filled with tears. "And you've been hiding from him, all this time?"

Abbie sobbed. "Yes, Papa. He found me once. I'm so afraid. I've been so afraid."

She began to weep wholeheartedly, and Papa wrapped his arms around her, pulling her into his lap as though she was a very little girl.

"Nothing is going to hurt you, Abbie." Papa's voice trembled with a fierce, abiding love. "Nothing is ever going to hurt you. I'm going to keep you safe." He kissed her forehead.

"How, Papa?" Abbie sobbed.

"You're going to stay right here inside the tenement," said Papa. "Gail and I have to go to work every day, but you'll be safe here. No one needs to know you're here. You can do the housework, and the cooking, and the mending – we'll be so glad of your help." He drew back a little, looking seriously into her eyes. "But you are not to set foot outside this tenement, never, not for anything. Do you understand?"

Abbie felt a twinge of discomfort at this idea, but it was drowned in an overwhelming rush of relief and gratitude. She knew that she trusted her father. He would keep her safe.

She hoped with all her soul that he would keep himself safe, too.

"I love you, Papa," she whispered.

Papa hugged her close to her chest. She listened to the steady thump of his heart, and she had never been so glad to be home.

※

IN A MATTER OF WEEKS, the home for which Abbie had yearned so wholeheartedly became little more than a prison.

She sat by the only little window, one of Papa's shirts draped over her lap as she slowly pieced together a small rip under the arm. It was a little task; the tear was so small that Papa hadn't even mentioned it, and Abbie had found it when she was washing his shirt. She would have been able to mend it in five minutes. Her convalescence had gone well, and she felt strong again now. Her nimble fingers were capable and skilled after years of mending dresses at the brothel.

Still, Abbie drew out the little task, her fingers working slowly, pausing at intervals to gaze out onto the street. It was so quiet out there during the day. Most people were at work or had gone to the richer areas to beg; only a few drunken old men were lying on the street corner, chortling at nothing, the coarse sound of their laughter reminding her too much of the brothel.

Abbie finished the last stitch and let out a sigh, glancing around the little room. The bed was made with military precision; every surface was scrubbed and polished to the best of her ability. There was just nothing to do in here.

Nothing at all.

She gazed out of the window, feeling both restless and lethargic somehow. After so many years of yearning to come home, Abbie found herself itching to leave it. Not for long, of course. Evenings with Papa and Gail were gloriously happy. But it was just past eleven in the morning, and they wouldn't be home for hours and hours.

Abbie found her heart quailing within her at the thought of spending another full day alone in this house with nothing to do. She knew that Papa just wanted to keep her alive, but this hardly felt like living.

Movement caught her eye across the street. She leaned closer against the window, her breath fogging the glass. A door had opened on the bottom of the tenement building opposite, and a young woman walked outside. It looked like a beautiful day, perhaps the first real sunshine of the spring, and the young woman was carrying a basket over her arm. Perhaps she was going out to find some food. Abbie knew full well that her shopping would be meagre: perhaps a loaf of bread, a few scraps of offal if she was lucky. But Abbie felt a powerful jealousy rise in her anyway, a deep desire to be that young woman who could walk in the sunlight.

She squinted a little, trying to make out which of her neighbors it was; she knew none of their names, but all of their faces. The young woman, however, had a scarf pulled over her head, probably to shield her ears from the crisp breeze that was whistling around the tenement despite the bright sun. Abbie tried to get a look, but even when the woman turned around and looked back, her face was wreathed in shadow.

The sight sparked an idea in Abbie's mind. She looked across the room, where Gail had left a faded shawl on the kitchen table. Abbie had planned on mending a tiny hole in it later that day. She got up quickly, went to the table and wrapped it over her head. Returning to the window, she squinted at her faint reflection in the glass.

If she arranged her hair just so, and tied the shawl just so, then no one would know her. Not even Leroy Hawkins.

The thought was a wild one, and it woke a trembling fear in the pit of her stomach, but the hope that leapt in her heart was by far greater than the fear. She squared her shoulders and looked up at the door. It would be so easy. Papa would never know she was gone…

She just needed to feel the sun on her face. She would go only as far as the end of the street, and then she'd come back.

Quickly, Abbie strode out of the front door. It felt delicious to stretch her legs out of the door again, and the sudden touch of the cold breeze on her face was like an unexpected kiss. The sun was glorious, dazzling her eyes slightly, and she held out her bare hands to feel it on her ashen skin.

It was so good to be moving, so good to draw fresh air into her lungs. And so, when Abbie reached the end of the street, she couldn't bring herself to stop.

CHAPTER 13

ABBIE HAD NEVER CONSIDERED the wharves to be beautiful before. There was so much poverty, after all, everywhere she looked; ragged children, big-eyed with starvation, begging on the street corners; vendors with ramshackle stalls, trying to eke out a living selling cigarette butts and bits of rag; rough-mouthed sailors with shaggy beards and wild eyes, passed out drunk in the middle of the street even though it was not yet midday. There was a pervasive aroma of fish lying over everything, holding a rotten edge to it.

But to Abbie, who had been staring at the same four walls for hours on end, this all felt like stepping straight into paradise.

She tipped back her head and took a deep breath of the nearly-fresh air, making sure to keep a hand clasped under her chin, the scarf wrapped tightly around her face. Even though she stuck to the streets she knew, not venturing more than a few blocks from the tenement, there was still so much to see. A lot had changed in four years. A new little market square had cropped up in what had once been a cul-de-sac of ramshackle houses, and there were a few courageous little shops in it, struggling to scrape out a living. There was a grocery, and a bakery, and, to Abbie's shock, a combined millinery and tailor.

She froze when she spotted the garments hanging in the window, saw the neat little man just behind the door, a tape measure draped over his shoulders, nodding and bowing to a customer as though the scruffy old sea-dog inside was a real gentleman. From what little Abbie could read, she gleaned from the sign outside that the tailor's prices were very cheap. That had to be why the little shop had survived for so long.

She knew she should turn back. Speaking to anyone, allowing anyone to lay eyes upon her face, could be a disastrous mistake – one that could endanger both her and her family. But she couldn't stop herself. As always, the sight of the tailor had sparked within her one last fragment of hope, hope for the only thing in this world that had ever given her hope for a happy future.

To risk her life for this one thing was better than to go on living without it.

She went up hesitantly to the front door; there was no back entrance, the shop was hardly bigger than their tenement. Pushing it open, she kept her eyes down, her scarf clutched tightly around her face as she approached the clerk in the back corner.

"Excuse me, sir," she quavered.

The clerk was writing measurements in a ledger as the tailor called them out as he ascertained the improbable proportions of the sea captain. "Yes?" he said, his tone bored.

"I... I was just wondering if... well... if the tailor has an assistant," said Abbie. She had to squeeze the word out past a growing lump in her throat; she trembled to the very tips of her toes. Oh, this hope was so foolish, and yet she hoped it so fervently...

The clerk stared at her. "What?" he said.

"I'm looking for someone I used to know, and he was a tailor's assistant," said Abbie, "but..."

The clerk gave her a disgusted look. "Go away," he said.

"Please, sir, I..."

"Go away." The clerk flapped a hand at her. "I don't have time for this."

Abbie wanted to plead with him, but the tailor was looking at her, and she was well aware of the dangers of calling attention to herself. She should never have come in here in the first place. What if her actions placed Papa or Gail in danger?

Fear and guilt strangled her. She wrapped her scarf more tightly around her face and hurried outside, tears burning her eyes. She should go home, straight home. She had been a terrible fool to leave the tenement at all. How could she endanger her family over this stupid hope that one day she would lay eyes on Robah again?

Weeping bitter tears as she stumbled down the street, Abbie promised herself, deep inside her heart, that she would give up. She would never go to a tailor's shop again. She would stay in the tenement like Papa had asked and forget that there had ever been real joy in her life.

Between her tears and her struggles to keep her face covered with the scarf, Abbie wasn't looking where she was going; in fact, she could hardly see at all. Choked by tears, she didn't see the man walking along the street until she bumped into him.

She knew it was a man at once. His smell surrounded her, and she heard him grunt deep in his chest as she rammed into him. Terror flooded her veins like mercury. Hawkins. It had to be him. He had found her, and in an instant, she would die with his blade in her throat.

She let out a scream and stumbled back, clutching at the scarf, looking around wildly, but her heel found a crack in the paving and she fell backwards, hard. Rattled and hurting, Abbie let out another yelp of total panic and tried to scramble to her feet, uncoordinated with fear.

"Miss. Miss. It's all right. Here – let me help you."

The voice somehow penetrated the dark fog of fear that had filled her mind. Abbie froze. It held such familiarity... but surely it couldn't be.

A warm hand wrapped around her own and lifted her gently to her feet. "I'm so sorry. I really should look where I'm going. Are you all right?"

Abbie looked up, not caring that the scarf was falling away from her face and found herself staring right into Robah's eyes.

"I'm so clumsy, I..." Robah fell silent. He was still holding Abbie's hand, and his eyes widened, then welled up instantly with tears.

Abbie wanted to throw her arms around him, to kiss him, to tell him again how much she loved him. But the desire brought back the memory of their last encounter, of their argument. She clutched his hand, terrified he would disappear before she could apologise.

"Robah, I'm so sorry," she said. "I'm so sorry I left things the way that I did. I'm sorry for the things I said, and for being so strange and driving you away, and…"

"Oh, Abbie." Robah's voice broke. "Oh, you could never drive me away."

He wrapped his arms around her and held her, delicately, as though she was made of something fragile and precious. He was shaking from head to toe, and Abbie hesitated only for a moment before she allowed herself to melt into his embrace. Her tears soaked into his coat, but he didn't seem to mind. He just held her and allowed her to weep.

"I thought you were… gone," Robah whispered. He pulled back at last, his arms still wrapped around her, and gazed down at her. "I went back to the brothel that Saturday morning. The tailor had fired me because of Mama. We were going further into the city to look for work, but I had to say goodbye. I felt so foolish that I'd allowed such a silly little argument to come between us… I brought you flowers." His voice broke. "But you weren't there. Lady Rose wouldn't say what had happened. Daisy told me that you had jumped from the window… that she'd heard you scream."

Abbie realised abruptly that her scarf was hanging over her shoulders. She drew back, clutching it, and wrapped it around her head.

"Abbie, please." Robah took a step closer. "Is this about that Leroy Hawkins? Please, tell me. I want to help you. I want to make it right."

"I can't," said Abbie. "You'd be in danger."

Robah's eyes flashed with something as warm and fierce as the expression in her father's face when she had told him.

"If you're in danger, I want to protect you," he said. "I don't care about danger. I just want the truth, Abbie." His eyes filled with vulnerability again. "I need to know the truth."

The pain in his voice was raw and real. Abbie's heart broke to think of the pain she had put him through for these four years, even though she was trying to protect him. She hung her head.

"It's a long story," she said. "Is there somewhere we can sit?"

※

There was a tiny, grubby courtyard at the back of the tailor's shop, where Robah did, indeed, work as an assistant. As it turned out, he had half an hour's precious time off for lunch. They sat on the floor of the courtyard with their backs against the wall, watching a few newly made garments dry on the washing line strung across it and sharing the chunk of bread that Robah had gone out to buy for lunch.

He listened silently, with wide, sorrowful eyes, as Abbie told him everything; the murder, the reason why she was so afraid of Hawkins' picture in the paper, her encounter with him in the brothel, her escape. When she told him about reaching her father's door, half-dead and starving, Robah put an arm around her shoulders and held her against him for a long time.

"I'm so sorry, Abbie," he whispered. "I had no idea."

"I should have told you. But I was so afraid for you." She bit her lip. "I'm still afraid for you, and for Papa, and for Gail..."

"Don't be afraid." Robah held her a little tighter. "I'm here for you. Don't worry."

"You can't tell your mama," said Abbie. "We can't put her in danger too."

Robah's smile held wistful sorrow. "She can never be in danger again," he said quietly.

"What do you mean?" Abbie stared at him, frightened. "Is... is Priscilla all right?"

"I'm afraid not. She died just a few months after you were gone," said Robah. "She was already sick when Lady Rose threw her out of the brothel, although she hid it well, even from you and me. I did my best, but she just wasted away in the end."

"I'm so sorry to hear that," said Abbie.

"She suffered so much, and in the end, she regretted so much," said Robah. "She was searching for so many answers all her life, but I believe she did find them before she died." His grip on her tightened. "I was so alone. I'm so glad you're here."

Abbie leaned her head against his shoulder, relief and a kind of exhausted joy filling her. "I'm so glad I found you," she whispered. "Now I can come to see you. I've been missing you so much."

"It's not safe for you to be out on the streets," said Robah gently. "I'll come and see you instead, when I have some time off."

"Yes." Abbie grinned. "Papa and Gail would love to meet you."

"Where do you live?" asked Robah.

"Hey. Boy!"

Abbie and Robah both jumped to their feet. The back door of the shop banged open, and the tailor was standing in the doorway, his tape measure still swinging around his neck. His eyes rested on Abbie and blazed with fury.

"Do you think I pay you to paw at wenches all day, boy?" he roared.

"He's not..." Abbie began.

"Get out of here." The tailor seized a broom as if he would chase her off with it like a stray cat. "Go away."

Robah squeezed Abbie's hand. "I'll see you another time," he said. "Go quickly – before you get into trouble."

Abbie wrapped her scarf around her face, backing toward the gate. Again, the words leapt from her, sweet and unexpected. "I love you," she said.

Robah gave her a dazzling smile before disappearing into the tailor's shop, but his words floated toward her over the tailor's yelling, lifting up her very soul.

"I love you, too."

※

ABBIE WAS SINGING as she set the table when Papa and Gail returned from work that evening. It felt a little strange to be setting a table in their tenement, but at least Abbie had learned how from Priscilla. The thought of the older woman's fate was saddening, but in a way, Abbie felt that Priscilla had been set free at last.

Papa gave his lovely, deep chuckle as he came into the tenement and hung his coat by the door. "Looks like you're expecting kings and queens to a banquet, darling," he said.

Abbie smiled over at him from her place by the hearth as she gave the stew a final stir. The table was far from extravagant; they had a few mismatched tin spoons and some wooden bowls, one of which had a crack in it that had to be stopped with one's finger if one was eating soup. Still, it looked neat and cosy, the three little places all set next to one another.

"You two are royalty to me," she said.

"That's so sweet of you to say." Gail came over to her and kissed her cheek. "How was your day?"

Wonderful, thought Abbie. But she didn't want Papa to know she'd gone outside; he would be angry, and frightened. She knew she would have to tell him. She'd have to return to the tailor at the first opportunity and tell Robah where to find her, but not tonight.

She had something important to ask him tonight.

"My day was all right," she said, carefully keeping her tone casual. "How about yours?"

"Just fine," said Gail. She smiled. "Mrs. Potts is starting to teach me a few bits of sewing."

"And how's your leg, Papa?" asked Abbie, scooping stew into his bowl.

Papa smiled in a way that was nearly carefree, the way he always did when she asked him. "Oh, I'm fine, pet," he said.

He always said that, and Abbie never believed him, but usually there had been very little that she could do. She squared her shoulders. Tonight, that would change. "Don't you think you need some liniment from the apothecary for that leg, Papa?"

Papa stared at her. "Oh, darling, don't worry about it," he said. "There's no money for that."

Abbie sat down beside him. "There could be," she said, "if I had a job."

Silence fell. Gail froze with her spoon halfway to her mouth.

Papa's eyes were filled with stern sorrow. "No," he said.

"Papa, please," said Abbie. "I could cover my face and find somewhere to work. I could..."

"It's too dangerous," said Papa flatly. "Abbie, what if that man sees you?" Pain filled his eyes.

"I know it could put you and Gail in danger," said Abbie quietly, "so I won't do it, if you don't want me to. But think how much better our lives could be, Papa. Wouldn't that be worth the risk?"

Papa's eyes hardened. "Maybe I would know, Abbie, if only you would tell me who the killer was."

Abbie felt the fight go out of her. She hung her head. "You know I can't do that."

Papa reached over the table and wrapped a big hand around Abbie's.

"I know this is difficult, my sweet, sweet child," he said softly. "But if you're too afraid to tell me the killer's name, then how can I protect you from him if you want to go out there? I'm sorry, but I'm not going to allow it."

Abbie nodded, fighting back the tears that were building in her eyes.

"Do you understand, my love?" said Papa.

Abbie did understand, but that didn't make it any easier. How was she going to see Robah now?

CHAPTER 14

THE TENEMENT HAD NEVER FELT SO small as it felt for the next few days.

Abbie leaned out of the open window, taking long, deep breaths as she gazed across the slum in the direction of the new little market square and the tailor shop that held the man she loved. She wanted with everything in her heart to go back there and speak to him, yet it had been just three days after her disagreement with Papa and leaving the tenement still didn't feel right. She felt guilty even for leaving it that once, even though the risk had so magnificently paid off.

She would have to get Papa to let her go outside if she wanted to introduce him to Robah. It would feel so wrong otherwise.

Propping her elbows on the windowsill, Abbie rested her chin in her hands and closed her eyes, remembering Robah's warm eyes, his smell, how perfectly her body had fit against his when he wrapped his arms around her. As precious as that thought was to her, it made it feel even more like the walls of the tenement were collapsing in around her. She wanted to

THE FISHMONGER'S DAUGHTER

run to him. To leap from this window, take wing somehow and soar over the rooftops until she reached his arms.

But she would have to wait.

At least she wouldn't be alone for so long today. It was a Saturday, and while Papa would spend the whole day working, the millinery closed at one o' clock. Gail would be home soon. In fact, Abbie could hear the front door opening, and she straightened up, pushing her sorrow out of her mind. She would have a precious afternoon with her dear sister now; she could try to forget her sorrows for a few hours.

Gail came into the tenement wreathed in sunshine, as she always was. "Hello, Abbie," she sang, striding inside, grasping Abbie by the hands and spinning her around once.

"You're in a good mood," Abbie laughed.

"Of course, I am." Gail flung herself down on the bed and gazed dreamily up at the ceiling. "I've had the most wonderful morning."

Abbie laughed, sitting down beside Gail. "Oh, do tell me about it," she said. "All of my mornings are the same."

Gail looked over at her, her eyes empathetic. "I know this must be so hard for you," she said.

"I feel trapped," Abbie admitted. She looked down at her feet, grateful that Gail was here. There were so many things that one could only tell a sister. "I'm so tired of being stuck in here."

"I know," said Gail. She sat up, resting a hand on her sister's shoulder. "But it's the only way to keep you safe."

"And to keep *you* safe," Abbie added, feeling a pang of guilt in the pit of her stomach. She was so glad she had seen Robah, but part of her was still chiding her for the possibility that her little expedition could have placed her father's and sister's lives in danger.

"I think Papa is being a little overprotective," Gail admitted. "It happened so long ago. How long are you going to hide? Forever?"

"You have a point," sighed Abbie. "I don't think I can do this forever."

"It's not much of a life," said Gail.

"And I'm a burden on the two of you," said Abbie.

"No." Gail wrapped her arms around her sister. "You're not a burden. Don't say that. We're so glad to have you here."

Abbie snuggled her face into the crook of Gail's neck. "I'm so glad I'm here with you," she whispered. "Now... let's be happy. Tell me about your day."

Gail sat back, giggling. "It was glorious." she said. "I met the most handsome man I've ever seen in all my life."

"Oh?" Abbie smiled.

"He's much older than I am, of course. And a gentleman. He came in with his lady friend, and he was so charming and witty, I nearly died." Gail giggled. "I know he's too old for me, and taken besides, but I felt it could do no harm to admire him from afar. He had the loveliest, chiseled features, like an old Greek statue."

"That sounds impressive," smiled Abbie, thinking of Robah's sweet, gentle face.

"And he had beautiful eyes – pale grey, like a snowy morning," said Gail. "I could have stared into them for hours. He smiled at me once and I just *melted*." She leaned back on the bed, kicking her feet in the air. "Oh, I'll probably never see him again, but I'll never forget his name. It rolls off the tongue so sweetly." She gave a girlish sigh. "Leroy Hawkins."

Abbie was on her feet before she could think, her back against the wall, her heart hammering with terror. "What?" she screamed.

Gail sat up, her eyes wide, turning very pale. "Abbie, what's wrong?" she said.

"Are you sure?" Abbie strode up to Gail, grabbing her arms and glaring into her eyes. "Tell me, Gail. Are you absolutely sure about that name?"

"Well – yes. He paid for the dress. I wrote it out in the ledger," said Gail, wide-eyed. "Why? What on Earth is the matter?"

Abbie's heart felt like it would leap from her chest. She grasped her sister and pulled her close, trembling violently. "Did he hurt you?"

"What? No." Gail pulled back. "Why would you think that?" Her eyes widened. "Oh... Abbie... don't tell me that he's... he's..."

Abbie didn't want her to guess. "Don't say it," she said. "Don't say anything. And don't ever go back to the millinery."

"But I have to," Gail protested. "It's the only way we can survive." She raised a trembling hand to her mouth. "I can't believe it. Abbie, is it really him? Is he the killer?"

Abbie's eyes filled with tears. Gail had been standing only a few feet away from the man who had destroyed Abbie's entire life, who posed an unrelenting threat to her family, and she hadn't even known it. She had giggled over him like any girl would giggle over a handsome gentleman, not knowing that even as he stood there, he was probably carrying a mortal weapon, ready to kill. For the first time, Abbie realised how she might be putting Gail in danger by failing to tell her.

"Yes," she whispered.

Gail turned very pale. She sat down abruptly on the bed and dropped her hands into her lap, where they trembled.

"He seemed so nice," she quavered.

"He's a monster, Gail," said Abbie, "and though he doesn't know it was you, he threatened your life."

Gail swallowed hard, but then rage came into her eyes. "You told me that the killer... grabbed you," she said, "in the brothel where you stayed."

Abbie turned her face away. That was another of the details that she hadn't told their father.

"Yes."

"I'll slap him," Gail growled. "If I ever see him again, I shall spit on his shoes."

"You'll do no such thing." Abbie seized Gail's hands. "Don't you understand what he could do to you?"

Gail looked up at her, wide-eyed. "I do," she whispered. "I do. But you have to understand, Abbie, I can't stop going to work. We'll starve."

"Then if you ever see him again, if he ever comes back, you must hide," said Abbie. "In case he sees the resemblance and guesses who you are. You must go to the back room and hide and never come out until he's gone."

Gail nodded vigorously. "I will. I promise."

"Good." Abbie let out a shaky breath. "I hope he never comes back."

"I'd never seen him before. I think the girl who came in was his new girlfriend," said Gail. "Maybe he won't come back. But if he does, Papa will deal with him. He'll be so angry when he finds out who it is."

"You can't tell him." Abbie cried.

Gail stared at her. "But you told me."

"I told you because you might bump into him again at the millinery," said Abbie. "But Papa... no gentleman would go down to the wharves where Papa works. There's no need for him to know. Don't you see, Gail? Papa would do something foolhardy if he knew."

"Maybe something foolhardy needs to be done," said Gail stubbornly.

"Don't say that." Abbie shuddered. "Oh, Gail, please, if you love me, you must promise not to tell Papa."

Gail gave her a troubled look. "I've never kept secrets from Papa before," she said softly. "I even told him about the time I kissed Jimmy Hamilton in the alley."

Abbie squeezed her hands. "But this time you have to promise me," she said.

Gail wavered. Then she dropped her eyes, hanging her head.

"All right," she murmured. "I promise."

THREE MORE DAYS TRICKLED PAST, in agonizing slowness and tremulous tension. Abbie had never felt an atmosphere like this in their tenement before. There had been suffering, so much suffering, but never this terseness, these false smiles, this tension in the air over supper. The conversation was so stilted. Gail kept shooting nervous glances at Abbie, and every time Abbie tried to steer the conversation in the direction of getting a job or a little more freedom, Papa was quick to change the subject.

Supper had always been Abbie's favorite time of the day; a welcome break from the intolerable silence and loneliness that every day brought for her. Now, though, as she stirred the pot of chicken broth she was making for supper, she found herself almost dreading Papa's and Gail's return.

Things had been so strange between them all that morning. She'd made each of them a slice of toast for breakfast, and Gail had been red-eyed and teary when Abbie had given her the toast. Abbie had asked her what was wrong, but Gail simply shook her head, forced a fake smile, and hurried out of the door.

"What's wrong with Gail, Papa?" Abbie asked, turning to her father and holding out the piece of toast wrapped in brown paper.

Papa had given her a long, quiet look that had held something stern and a little bit frightening; something that used to come into his eyes when he regaled them as little children with tales of his adventures on the seven seas.

"Everything is all right, pet," he'd said at length. He had wrapped his arms around her then, and she had felt him trembling. "There is nothing I would not do for you," he had added. "Nothing. I could lay down my life for you and not regret it."

"Papa?" Abbie had been shocked. "What are you talking about?"

"Nothing." Papa had not smiled. "I just want you to know how much I love you."

Then they both had left, and Abbie had sat in the tenement with her fears and confusion, all alone.

Now, though, exhausted from a day's worrying, Abbie wasn't sure she was ready to face another strange and awkward family meal. She wished everything could go back to the way it had been before she had seen Hawkins murder that man. They had been hungry then, but they had been a family.

She heard the front door squeaking and braced herself, forcing a smile onto her face. She was the one who had broken this family, and she would be the one to pick up the pieces.

Gail came in a few moments later, looking tired and pale. Abbie straightened up, smiling widely. "Hello, Gail," she said. "I'm glad you're back."

"Is Papa here?" Gail asked.

Abbie shook her head. "Not yet. Didn't he walk with you, like he normally does?"

"No... no. Not tonight," said Gail. "He usually meets me at the crossroads."

Abbie shrugged, trying to quell a strange unease in the pit of her stomach. "I'm sure he's all right. It's only a quarter past six now – he's often only home around half past, if he had some late customers."

"Yes, I'm sure you're right." Gail sounded unconvinced. "Sometimes I pass by the crossroads early, and he's always told me not to wait for him."

"The broth could boil for a few more minutes in any case." Abbie put the lid back on the pot. "Why don't you sit down and have some tea? I'll put the kettle on."

"Yes… all right." Gail sat down, but she was fidgeting, her eyes darting outside, then down to the floor.

Abbie made the tea quickly, taking deep breaths. It was early. Papa often was not yet home at this time. So why did she feel so passionately worried about him?

"Here you are," she said, giving Gail the tea and sitting down on the bed beside her.

"Thank you." Gail stared down into it as if she had never seen tea before.

Abbie put a hand on her knee. "How did your day go?" she asked.

"Oh, fine. Everything is fine." Gail said the words with a false, brittle brightness.

Abbie squeezed her knee gently. "I know it's not, Gail, not really," she said. "Won't you tell me what's wrong? You seem so worried and jumpy today. It's scaring me."

Gail bit her lip, tears welling up in her eyes.

"Gail?" Abbie put an arm around her shoulders. "What's going on?"

"Oh, Abbie, you'll be so angry." Gail covered her face with her hands and began to sob. "But I had to tell him. I had to, I had to, and now he's in the most awful danger."

THE FISHMONGER'S DAUGHTER

"He?" Abbie's heart thumped nastily. "Papa?"

"Yes. It's my fault. It's all my fault." Gail was crying wholeheartedly. "I think something awful has happened to him."

"What kind of awful?" Abbie was trembling.

"He kept on going on about how he wished you would tell him who the killer was," Gail cried. "He wanted to know so much... and I... I'm no good at lying. He knew. He knew and he begged and begged me to tell him, and I thought it was the right thing. I thought it was what I should do." She looked up at Abbie. "Oh, please, Abbie, forgive me."

"Don't mind that now. What did you tell him?" said Abbie urgently, remembering their conversation that morning.

"I told him it was Leroy Hawkins," said Gail. Tears coursed down her cheeks. "Oh, Abbie, I,,, I think he's done something terrible."

"Something terrible?" Abbie whispered, her mouth dry.

"I think he's gone after him," said Gail.

Abbie felt cold down to the tips of her toes. She trembled, staring at Gail. "What are you talking about? What happened?"

"I told him last night when we were walking home. He was so angry," said Gail. "Not with you, or with me... but he went all white and quiet the way he does when he's truly angry. And then he said that he might be home late. I begged him not to do it. I knew he wanted to. He didn't deny he was going to go after Hawkins. He just said that he would do whatever he had to do for his girls."

Abbie felt a hot tear run down her own cheek. If only she had known, she could have stopped him earlier this morning...

"What are we going to do?" Gail sobbed.

"There's only one thing we can do." Abbie got up, her movements cold and mechanical. She lifted the pot from the fire and put it on the table, then reached for her coat behind the door. "We're going to find him."

"But you can't go out," said Gail.

Abbie turned to her sister, trembling with shame, fear, and anger. "We're going to find him, Gail," she spat.

She strode out of the door before anyone could stop her.

CHAPTER 15

"What if he's not here?"

Gail voiced Abbie's fear as they walked quickly along the wharves, muffled in their coats despite the still summer night. Dusk had fallen, and even the familiar shadows of the wharves seemed warped and twisted, as if they had morphed into demons at the retreat of the sun.

Abbie hadn't known where to start looking, so she had led Gail to the spot where Papa usually sold fish, hoping to find some kind of a lead.

"He'll be there. He has to be," she said, terrified to contemplate the alternative. "Maybe he didn't go through with it. Maybe he's still selling fish."

Gail's voice was small and scared. "People don't buy fish in the dark, Abbie."

"It's not quite dark yet," said Abbie, wrapping her arms tightly around herself. She shivered.

Papa's fish-selling spot was a corner right down by the docks, and it had been the same place for many years. Abbie quickened her step as they came closer. Her heart was pounding in her chest as they turned the corner.

Papa wasn't there.

The streetlight shone down onto his usual place, rich and golden, but there was no sign of her father.

"Oh, Abbie." Gail was crying. "What are we going to do?"

Abbie covered her mouth with her hands, trembling, trying frantically to think of something. What if he had gone to teach Hawkins a lesson? Where would he go? Abbie had no idea where Hawkins lived, or whether he had come down to the wharves. There was no way to even start searching for her father.

And if he really had gone after Hawkins, then chances were that he was dead by now, floating down the Thames with a cut throat, another nameless body in the paper tomorrow morning...

The world spun around her, darkness filling her vision. She felt her knees wobble. She had just gotten Papa back. She couldn't lose him again... not again.

"Abbie?" Gail grabbed her arm.

Abbie somehow managed to stay upright, clutching at her sister. "We have to find him, Gail," she whispered. "He has to be alive. Oh, Papa, Papa, he has..."

Gail froze beside her. "There's someone here," she quavered.

The girls both turned to see two figures coming up the street toward them. In the dusk, their movement was strange, lurching, lopsided, and for an awful moment Abbie believed she was looking right into the face of that terrifying phantom of death that had been following her for so many years. But when they stepped out into the light, she saw that it was two men. The younger of them was ashen pale, blood dripping down the side of his face from a cut in his cheek, but he was courageously supporting another man with an arm over his shoulders, who was half limping, half being dragged.

Abbie and Gail stared, frozen to the spot.

The younger man didn't seem to notice them. He was gasping for breath. "Almost there," he grunted, seeming to be heading for Papa's fish-selling spot. "Almost there, George."

"George," Abbie breathed. It was their father's name.

The two men made it to the lamplit corner, and the younger one half knelt down, half collapsed onto the sidewalk. The elder fell onto the ground and rolled over, and the lamplight hit his face, and Abbie let out a moan that seemed to tear apart every fibre of her being.

It was Papa, and he had now passed out, his face a mask of blood.

Gail was beside him before Abbie could move, cupping his face in her hands, her voice choked with tears. "Papa. Oh, Papa. Wake up. Say something. Please, Papa."

Abbie stumbled closer and fell to her knees beside Papa. He was lying very still, breathing in shallow gasps. She grasped his hand; his arm flopped loosely, and his knuckles were covered in dried blood. She didn't know whose it was.

"Are you his ... his daughters?" rasped the younger man. He sat back, slumped against the streetlamp, an arm wrapped around his ribs. He looked ready to pass out, too.

"Yes," Gail sobbed.

"What happened?" Abbie cried.

He sucked in a breath and winced. "When he came up to the ship this morning, he asked us to help him with a problem. L-Leroy Hawkins. We were h-happy to help... at least, I thought we all were happy to help. We agreed to meet at the pub where Hawkins drinks most nights and teach him a lesson." The young man drew in another painful breath; a trickle of blood bubbled at his lips. "All the men said ... they'd come. But when we got there, it was only George and me."

"You're hurt," said Gail. "Abbie, he's hurt bad."

The young man ignored her. "Hawkins... was inside. Your father... he just wouldn't go back. I tried to persuade him. But he... he wanted justice. He said the man had stolen years from your lives. So we went inside and went for Hawkins... but he had a knife..." The young man lifted his hand and touched his chest briefly.

"Was m-my papa stabbed?" Abbie sobbed.

"No. The knife... He got me." The young man gave a choked laugh, and a thin line of blood ran down his chin. "George punched Hawkins twice, hard. But Hawkins is younger... quicker. George fell... Hawkins was kicking him and kicking him... then the bobbies came. I didn't know where he lived... hoped you would... be here."

The young man's voice was gurgling now, as if he were drowning in blood, just like that man in the alley, the man Hawkins had killed four years ago. Abbie was blind with tears. She wanted to save him, but she knew she couldn't, just like she couldn't save that man in the alley.

"Mister? Mister?" Gail squeaked.

"It's... all... right," the man whispered, his voice scratchy. "No one... will miss... me."

He let out a last sigh, a gush of blood running out of his mouth.

"No. No. *No*. It can't be. It can't. Please don't die," Abbie pleaded, but it was too late. She leaned closer to him. "Thank you, Mister. Thank you."

She hoped he heard it, before his soul took wing and left his broken body behind on the street corner.

꧁꧂

IT WAS hard to tell where Papa's old scars ended, and new wounds began. He had always been a man of unparalleled dignity, even in this tiny, grubby tenement, and it felt so strange to Abbie to see so much of him.

He had come to, but even so, carrying him home had been nearly impossible. They had draped his arms over their shoulders and stumbled onward, but Gail was taller than Abbie, and so Papa had listed horribly sideways as they walked. Still, they had made it and laid him upon the bed, where he quickly passed out again. Gail was still crying quietly for the young man who had given his life to save Papa.

Now they had stripped him to his underwear, and they were slowly bathing his many, many wounds in warm water. There seemed to be cuts and bruises all over him. One side of his chest was almost black with bruising; his left arm moved strangely, bonelessly, and there was a nasty, grinding sound from inside it. Abbie bound it up as well as she could.

"He needs a doctor," whispered Gail, her eyes round with terror.

Abbie knew. But she also knew it would be a long time before Papa could sell fish again, and that they would be lucky to pay the rent and eat. A doctor was out of the question.

They dressed him in clean linen nightclothes, and Abbie applied a cold compress to the big round lump on Papa's left temple. It looked unbelievably painful, but his face was pallid and motionless. She kept one hand on his chest to feel the reassuring rise and fall of his breathing.

"I did this." Gail was sitting on the other side of the bed. Tears had been pouring continuously down her face all evening. "Oh, Abbie, I should never have told him."

Abbie looked up at her, her anger flaring. "You promised, Gail."

"I know. But he begged." Gail covered her face with her hands and cried hopelessly. "I'm so sorry, Abbie," she moaned, her voice muffled. "I should never have told him. I didn't know this would happen. I never meant for this to happen."

Her heart-wrenching sobs overwhelmed Abbie, and she hung her head, deeply ashamed. "I know. You would never want something like this to happen to Papa," she said. "It's not your fault, Gail. It's... it's mine."

Gail looked up. "How can it be yours?" she sobbed.

"I'm the one who came back." Abbie felt tears building in her eyes as she looked at her sister. "I should never have come. I should have left you alone to be safe and happy without me."

"No."

The voice was a weak little croak, but it was the most wonderful sound that Abbie had ever heard. She looked down to see that Papa was struggling to open the one eye that was not swollen shut. He looked up at her, his gaze unfocused.

"No," he whispered. "We could never have been happy without you, Abbie. We're so glad you're back."

"Papa," Gail cried. She looked as though she wanted to throw herself upon his chest, but she grasped his hand instead and stroked it. "Oh, Papa, we were so frightened."

"Why did you go after him?" Abbie sobbed.

"I-I wanted him to know that h-he'd chosen the wrong family to threaten." Papa shifted, a muscle jumping in his cheek as he gritted his teeth with pain. "I don't think Hawkins has ever been s-struck the way I struck him."

"Oh, Papa, but he hurt you," whispered Abbie.

"And your friend..." Gail stopped.

Papa's eye filled with sadness and his voice grew stronger. "Abe deserved better. But I'm still glad I went after him. We both knew what could happen. And I don't regret it." He looked up at Abbie. "I had to try, my darling. I-I had to try something, anything, to keep you safe. I have no regrets."

Abbie squeezed his hand, pressing the compress back against his temple. "Rest, Papa," she whispered.

Papa may not have any regrets, but his actions had done no good at all. Hawkins was still out there. And now he knew she was still alive.

"Abbie..." Papa seemed to be drifting off again.

"Yes?"

He made a valiant effort to open both eyes, grimaced, and closed them instead.

"You can never set foot outside this tenement again," he said. "Not as long as Hawkins is out there. Do you hear me? We didn't hurt him... He can come after you."

Abbie thought of Robah and felt her heart ripping. If she couldn't leave, she'd never see him again. But Papa was so hurt. She couldn't risk that happening again.

She hung her head, tears dripping off the end of her nose.

"Yes, Papa," she whispered. "I promise." And this time, she meant it.

PART IV

CHAPTER 16

Two Years Later

THE BLEAK WIND seemed to slice through Abbie's threadbare coat like a thrown knife. It was hard to believe that the almanac said it was spring now; the sleet that tore against the side of Abbie's scarf felt like the bitter peak of winter. It seemed as though every gust of wind, every stinging handful of sleet was meant just for her. As if the world itself hated her.

Perhaps she was only thinking this way because of the chilblains on her feet and the chapped, cracked skin on the back of her hands and the steady hunger gnawing at the pit of her stomach. But it was hard not to think so, as Abbie stood on one side of the marketplace, staring at what had once been the tailor's shop where Robah had worked.

There was nothing left of it now. Just a sad, empty building, like every other shop on this optimistic little market square.

The windows were all boarded up, and the *For Sale* sign had grown old and chipped and faded.

She wondered if Robah thought she hated him. Perhaps he thought she was dead, and that would be better somehow, even though she could hardly bear the thought of him grieving her, giving up on her, and moving on with a new girl who wouldn't keep on leaving him like this.

But he was gone now. For better or worse, he had left her life, and she knew that this time she would never get him back. She would try to see that last afternoon with him as a precious and final gift, and not a tantalizing foretaste of what could have been.

Abbie turned around and limped back along the street. After two years of not leaving the tenement, her limbs still felt weak and shaky after even a few steps of walking, and it wasn't long before she had to sit down on the front step of an abandoned warehouse. She gazed around at the bleak street, muffled figures hurrying along it, empty buildings staring at her with the hollow eyes of broken windows. She had dreamed of this day for so long, the day that she could finally leave the tenement again and walk openly in the city. Tugging her scarf back over her face, she couldn't fight back her disappointment.

This was not what she had imagined.

Papa had never gone back to selling fish. Just when his wounds began to heal, a terrible fever took him, and he lay quiet for so long that Abbie gave up on ever looking into his eyes again. Ever since then, while he could stand and walk about a little now, he had been unable to work. Poor Gail had found a second job as a seamstress, and after coming home from work, she sat by the window in the failing light and together, they sewed dresses until midnight.

It had kept them alive, even though sometimes Abbie believed that being tortured with this guilt was worse than death. While her little sister had worked her fingers to the bone, stoic and uncomplaining, Abbie sat at home with her ailing father and tried her best not to lose her mind.

That had all changed last night. Gail had come home pale and exhausted as always, and she sat by the window with a dress she was sewing. She raised a needle and thread to the light and tried to thread the needle. She had tried again and again and again, then finally pricked her finger and burst into tears. It was then that she finally admitted the truth to George and Abbie: Her eyesight was fading, strained too much by hours of working in near darkness. It wouldn't be long before she couldn't sew at all anymore.

So here Abbie was, out on the street, crouched on the front step of this warehouse to catch her breath. She had seldom been so hungry in all her life, and she had forgotten how cold the wind really could be. And still no one had hired her. She knew she was risking her life and Papa's and Gail's by being out here, but the alternative was to starve. Hawkins' knife seemed kind by comparison.

She would have to keep trying. Trembling with weakness, she hauled herself to her feet and stumbled on, heading for the nearest slop shop. Maybe the proprietor needed a slopworker.

Maybe miracles really did happen. But Abbie had seen so few of them in her life.

It made it so hard to believe.

PAPA WAS COUGHING AGAIN. Abbie could hear him as she walked into the front door and turned into their little tenement. The sound was awful, red and raw, just like Mama had sounded in her final weeks, and it struck fear right into the pit of her stomach.

"Papa?" Abbie pushed the door open. "Are you all right?"

Papa was huddled in a blanket in front of the fire. They had long since sold the bed; he perched on the edge of a sleeping pallet now, which Abbie was quite sure was infested with bedbugs. Looking up at her, he gave her a watery smile. She was struck again by how much he had aged in two years. The strong-limbed titan that he once had been was replaced by a shell of an old man, his hairline receding, his face deeply lined with suffering.

"Oh, hello, Abbie," he said. "Any luck?"

"Answer my question first, Papa," said Abbie, hooking the kettle onto the fire.

"That won't do you much good, I'm afraid." Papa cleared his throat painfully. "There's no tea."

"I'm sure Gail will bring us some," said Abbie, with an optimism she did not feel.

"Rent's due tomorrow." Papa gave another awful, raw cough. "I doubt it."

Abbie's stomach cried out inside her. She wished she could get her hands on a whole chicken and some potatoes and carrots and rice. She wanted to make her papa the huge, wholesome, healthy meals she had made for the prostitutes at the brothel. Some of them had been spiteful women; all of them had had questionable morals. Yet she had fed them so well. Now she was looking at her papa, one of the best people she had ever known, a man of total integrity, total loyalty, and she couldn't even make him a cup of tea.

She turned away so that he would not see her tears. "Maybe we still have some coffee," she said, reaching for the box where they were once again keeping all of their things. Her hands were shaking. She knew there was none, and that Papa was growing thinner by the day. Would she have to watch him waste away?

A fat tear splashed down her cheek and landed on the wood, leaving a dark circle. Abbie pushed their few belongings around, searching for something: coffee, sugar, or just a scrap of hope.

It was hope that she found, but not in the box. It was in the slam of the front door. Gail hadn't slammed the door open that way in years, not since Hawkins had beaten their father to within an inch of his life, and it made both Papa and Abbie jump.

"What's gotten into your sister?" Papa muttered, looking up.

But the footsteps coming toward the tenement door were not Gail's, or at least, they were not only Gail's. There was a second set of steps; these were heavy, thumping, masculine.

Abbie's heart ground to a halt in her chest. She breathed heavily, terror thrilling through her.

"Abbie..." Papa began.

"Don't move." Abbie took the kettle from the fire. It wasn't very hot yet, but when she weighed it in her hand, it was heavy. It would have to do as her only weapon. She stepped in front of her father, trembling from head to toe. She knew Hawkins would kill her. But she had to try.

The door slammed open. Gail let out a shriek, and Abbie raised the kettle, prepared to deal a mighty blow –

"Abbie. Abbie!" The man in the door threw up his hands. "It's me."

Abbie dropped the kettle. Warm water splashed across her feet, and the kettle rolled across the floor. She could hardly believe her eyes as she stared at the tall, strong, ruddy man in the doorway. He had a rich red beard curling around his jaw, and his skin had a strong, brazen tan; but his eyes were still the same, deep brown, clever and loving, warm and kind.

"Patrick?" Abbie gasped.

"Sister." Patrick strode across the floor and enveloped her in a gigantic hug that seemed to crush every one of her bones.

"Oh... oh." Abbie clutched her brother. He smelled of sea salt and tar, and he was so strong and warm and solid in her arms. "I can't believe it's you."

Patrick let her go, staring down at her, and Abbie laughed with tears running down her cheeks. He looked so strong, so well; he wore a sodden white shirt rolled up at the sleeves and open at the neck, revealing a tangle of crimson chest hair.

"You look so well." she said.

"I am well," he said. His eyes softened then, and he laid a big hand on her cheek. "But Gail tells me that it hasn't been well with all of you."

Gail appeared behind Patrick. "He was walking home from the wharves," she said. "I saw him and nearly bowled him over in the street." Her eyes were wet. "Oh, Abbie, he's back."

A soft voice came from behind Abbie. "Son," Papa croaked.

Abbie stepped aside. When Patrick saw their father, his shoulders slumped, and tears glittered instantly in his eyes.

"Oh, Papa," he whispered.

"Son." Papa was laughing, his eyes aglow for the first time in years. Slowly, he rose, holding out his arms. "Oh, son, I'm so proud of you."

Patrick walked into Papa's arms like a little boy, and their father held him, sobbing. Abbie couldn't hold back. She wrapped her arms around both of them, and Gail joined them so that they were a circle of total love.

The family was together again.

And yet, even now, holding her long-lost family, Abbie still felt incomplete.

CHAPTER 17

Gail and Papa had long since gone to bed. It was nearly midnight, and Abbie was sitting in the front door of the tenement building, her feet on the sidewalk, gazing down the empty street. For years, this had been the only freedom she had ever had. Today, she had gotten to walk beyond this door for the first time in ages. Yet she still yearned for this breath of fresh air in the depth of the night, when no one was around to see her.

She closed her eyes, allowing the icy wind to lift her hair away from her neck and soothe her tired skin. It was so cold, but she couldn't bring herself to go back inside.

A quiet footstep sounded behind her. "Abbie?" said Patrick.

Abbie looked up. "Did I wake you?" she whispered.

"No, no. It's just impossible to sleep on that pallet with everyone else." Patrick sat down beside her, resting his big, callused hands on his knees. "I thought rolling around in a bunk was bad enough, but this…" He shook his head, his eyes haunted. "I had no idea that things had gotten this bad, Abbie."

"Papa wouldn't let us tell you," said Abbie. "He wanted you to spread your wings."

"I wish he had called me home, and that we'd been in contact more. I know he didn't know exactly where I was," said Patrick. "I've had good adventures, but I've missed you all so much. I'm sorry I was gone for so long."

"You didn't know," said Abbie.

"Well, I do now," said Patrick.

The sleet had stopped. They sat in silence for a few moments; Abbie looked up but could see no stars.

"How long are you staying?" she asked quietly.

Patrick gave her a surprised look. "What do you mean?"

"Well, I'm sure you're going out to sea again soon," said Abbie.

"No." Patrick shook his head. "Oh, Abbie, I couldn't possibly leave all of you like this. Not with Papa the way he is. He's so... so sickly." Patrick gave a shaky little sigh. "My wages will help support us for a little while; I've saved them all. I'll find work in the city, too."

"I've been trying," said Abbie. "Well, only for a day..." She paused. Papa had told him all about the business with Hawkins.

"No. You should stay safe." Patrick wrapped an arm around Abbie's shoulders. "I'm not going to let anything happen to my little sister. And I think I should try to find out more about this Hawkins character."

"No." Abbie pulled back, shaking her head violently. "Please, Patrick, don't even say his name... don't even read the papers if he's in them. I don't want what happened to Papa to happen to you." Tears filled her eyes. "He hasn't been the same since, and we... we need you."

"Ah, Abbie, it's all right." Patrick wrapped his arms around her. "I'm not going to do anything to put any of us in danger. I promise."

Abbie buried her face in his chest, weeping quietly. Patrick held her with such strong, steady arms. He reminded her so much of Robah, but he wasn't Robah, and she knew that she would never see him again.

But perhaps having Patrick home could be enough.

PATRICK'S RETURN immediately made things better, and not only because with his wages, as now they could have real meals two or three times a day. Patrick had been saving every penny for years, failing to indulge in grog and women the way so many of his shipmates did, and now he had even managed to get their bed back.

It was good to wake up in a real bed again, but it was even better to see the difference in Papa. It was as if Patrick woke something inside him that had long been sleeping, and at night the two men would sit in front of the fire, swapping stories of the open sea. Patrick's tales lit a fire inside, and Papa started to grow stronger. His cough even began to fade.

Gail also never sat up until midnight making dresses anymore; Patrick made sure of that. Instead, Abbie was able to find a little mending work, and her brother took care of the collections and deliveries.

Things were better than they had been for a very long time, and yet as Abbie sat by the window working on a man's shirt that she was mending, she still couldn't help feeling absolutely empty. Winter had finally relinquished its death grip on the city, and there were bits of greenery now wherever Abbie looked; buds on the London plane tree; a few scraps of weeds straggling up in the courtyard of a nearby shop; a struggling flower in a window-box across the street. New life was everywhere, but her heart felt old and shrivelled.

She turned her gaze back to her work, reminding herself how grateful she was to be contributing to the household at last. Gail was out at work, and Papa had actually gone out for a walk to get some fresh air for the first time in years. The doctor that Patrick had paid for had suggested it, and Abbie could see him strolling along the sidewalk now. His limp was worse than it had ever been, but he was plugging along with a determination Abbie hadn't seen in him for a long time.

Feet clumped on the passage outside, and Abbie looked up to see Patrick coming into the tenement. "How did it go?" she asked.

"Ah, hopefully good," said Patrick. "The lady is looking for a gardener, but she was hoping for someone with more experience. Still, she says she'll speak to her husband, and send me a note tomorrow."

"Good," said Abbie. She turned back to the window. "Just look at him, Patrick. He looks like the papa I know again."

Patrick joined her by the window. "I still feel so bad about everything you've all gone through," he said. "It should never have happened."

"It's not your fault." Abbie leaned against him. "I'm just so glad you're home."

"You don't seem glad, though," said Patrick gently.

Abbie looked up at him, surprised. "Oh, Patrick." she said. "I love you, and I'm so happy that…"

"I don't mean it like that." Patrick grabbed a wobbly three-legged stool from its spot by the fire and pulled it over, sitting down beside her. "I know you're glad I'm here. But something's bothering you, sister." He laid a hand on her knee. "Won't you tell me what it is?"

Abbie dropped her eyes. "It's silly," she said.

"I don't care," said Patrick. "I want to know."

"If you're so sure." Abbie bit her lip. "I… I… well, I'm missing someone. Someone I knew… back when I was cooking for the brothel." Robah was the only part of her story she hadn't told anyone.

"Oh?" Patrick gave her a gentle smile. "A young man?"

"Yes." Abbie felt her face growing warm. "He and his mother were the only people who were really kind to me in that time, Patrick. He was a gentleman when I was surrounded by pigs. He never laid a hand on me, not unless I reached for him first. He… he told me that he loved me. But when I left the brothel, I didn't see him again for two years, until I found him in a market square nearby about two years ago."

"So where is he now?" asked Patrick.

"That's the trouble." Tears burned in Abbie's eyes. "I don't know. I last saw him right before Papa was beaten up… I didn't even tell Papa and Gail about him because I sneaked out and Papa would have been so angry."

"Oh, Abbie," said Patrick.

"I went there the day you came home, to see if he was still working where I last found him. He was a tailor's assistant," said Abbie. "But the whole shop was gone. Boarded up. There was no one there." She looked up at him with tears in her eyes. "I'll never find him, Patrick. And I loved him. I really did. I wanted to spend the rest of my life with him. He was going to save me from the brothel."

"You don't know that you won't find him." Patrick wrapped his hands around hers.

"Yes, I do." Abbie turned her face away. "I can't. I've tried, but I can't even read. There's nothing I can do."

"But *I* can read," said Patrick. He squeezed her hands. "And I'll help you find him."

Abbie stared at him. "Do you mean it?"

"Of course, I do." Patrick smiled. "I just want to see all of you happy. And you've been through so much, my sweet sister. I'll do anything to help you."

"Patrick, thank you." Abbie put aside her mending and wrapped her arms around her brother's neck. "Oh, thank you so much for coming home."

"I can't promise anything, except to do my best," said Patrick.

Abbie felt hope spark in her heart for the first time in years. It flooded her veins, warm and alive, and she wept with the beauty of it.

"It's enough," she said.

CHAPTER 18

THE ONLY TREE that Abbie could see from the tenement had turned richly red and gold with the end of fall. Its leaves were falling slowly, dripping from the branches like tears, and lying at the roots of the tree in rich profusion. The branches were left bare and stark against the greying sky, and Abbie knew that it wouldn't be long before they were coated with frost and snow.

She had spent so many hours gazing at that tree. Her mending was done; it lay to one side, folded neatly, and yet there were still many hours left in the day. She would have to spend a few more hours trying not to lose her mind, trying to think of ways to be happy here in this tenement. She had so many reasons to be happy; she was safe, and warm; she had a happy, healthy family; there was a table and chairs in here again. Papa was selling fish again, his vivacity reignited by Patrick's return all those months ago. Patrick, too, had found work sweeping the street; it paid poorly, but it was something. Gail was courting a young man named Steven...

The world was moving on, living and loving, and Abbie was not.

She forced herself to get up from her seat by the window. Sitting by the window would do nothing for her. She had to accept it; Patrick had been searching for Robah for months, and he had come up empty every time, even though he could read. There was no Robah Carter in London. Perhaps he had left for greener pastures. Perhaps for the greenest pastures of them all. The thought made tears build in her eyes, but she blinked them back fiercely and picked up the pail that stood in the corner. She had scrubbed the floor yesterday, but she would scrub it again, if it would stop her from thinking about everything she had lost.

※

ABBIE SMELT PATRICK coming before she saw him, and the smell surprised her. She knew it was her brother's footsteps on the hallway outside, but he normally smelled of sweat and dust – the unhappy lot of the London street-sweeper. Instead, tonight, she could smell something hot and delicious and salty.

Gail looked up from where she was sipping a cup of tea by the kitchen table. "What's that smell?" she asked.

Papa was polishing his boots by the fire. "It smells like fried fish," he said. "And chips."

"Who can afford that in our tenement?" said Abbie, puzzled.

The front door swung open, and Patrick strode inside, holding up a parcel wrapped in newspaper like it was some kind of trophy. He wore a massive grin, lighting up the cold little room. Outside, the skies were low and grey, threatening the first snow of the season.

"I have wonderful news," he said.

"You have wonderful food," gasped Gail, almost drooling. "Is that what I think it is?"

Patrick deposited the parcel on the kitchen table and unrolled it, beaming. "Fish and chips," he said. "It's still good and hot."

"Patrick," gasped Abbie. "Where did you get this?"

"From the fish-and-chip shop, of course." Patrick's eyes were dancing mischievously.

"But how could you afford this? It'd cost a fortune, by our standards," said Papa.

"Our standards have just been raised, Papa." Patrick laughed, his eyes shining. "I've been given a new job. I'm going to be a clerk at the printer's."

"A clerk?" gasped Papa, his eyes shining. "Why, that's a job for a man of learning."

"I spent a little time bettering my mind on my travels." Patrick laughed. "And combined with Gail's wages, and your fish sales – well, we can move to a better tenement at last."

"That's glorious news." Abbie hugged her brother tightly. "Oh, Patrick, I'm so glad you're here."

"I'm glad to be here," said Patrick warmly. "Now – less talk, and more eating this wonderful fish, in the knowledge that it won't be our last good meal."

"Yes," said Gail, reaching for a chip.

THE FISHMONGER'S DAUGHTER

"Wait," said Abbie. "Let's put it onto plates." She giggled, giddy with the good news. "We're going to be fancy now, after all."

Papa laughed as Gail pouted. "Whatever makes you happy, darling."

Abbie took two coarse wooden plates from the box and scooped the chips into one and the fish into the other. Grabbing the newspaper, she balled it up – and that was when she saw the name.

R. Carter.

Abbie felt her heart kick in her chest. It couldn't be. There had to be a thousand Carters in London. How many of them could be called Roy, Ryan, Richard?

Her eyes scrabbled across the rest of the text, but she could decipher none of it. She only knew the shape of Robah's name because she had memorized it once during a bored afternoon at the brothel; Priscilla had written it down for her and shown her how to draw a heart around it. It was still the only thing she could read and write.

"Abbie?" Papa was looking at her with fear in his eyes. "What is it?"

"Is it... is it *him*? Is it... *Hawkins*?" Gail almost whispered.

"No," said Abbie. "No, it's not." She felt tears filling her eyes as she fought against her hope. "Patrick," she croaked.

"What is it?" asked Patrick.

"What does this say?" Abbie pushed the greasy paper toward him and pointed to that name, *R. Carter*, that might or might not be everything she had ever dreamed of.

165

Patrick smoothed it open on the table, his brow furrowing briefly before a smile crossed his face. "Abbie... I think... I think it might..." he began.

Abbie was trembling. "Please," she said. "Just read it."

"*Residents of the wharves will be pleased to know that a new tailor is opening on Cornwall Street,*" Patrick read. "*The proprietor, R. Carter (20), will be open for business next week.*"

"A tailor," Abbie breathed. "A tailor... and he has the same initial... and last name."

"What?" said Gail, nonplussed.

"How old is the paper?" said Abbie urgently.

"It's two weeks old," said Patrick, checking the header. "But that doesn't matter. It's there, in the cul-de-sac that you told me about."

"What are you talking about?" asked Papa.

Abbie sat down abruptly, her body trembling with the effort of not hoping too much. But oh, the hope was rising in her, overwhelming her, and she couldn't hold back its terrible tide, no matter how much she feared it would soon be turned to utter agony.

Patrick laid a hand on hers. "I think we might have found the person Abbie loves," he said quietly.

"You have a beau?" gasped Gail. "Abbie, tell me everything."

"How?" said Papa, wide-eyed.

"Oh, I met him long before I came home," said Abbie. "He's so kind and sweet and clever..."

She told them about Robah and tried not to hope. But it was a losing battle.

❦

THEY WERE ONLY a block away from R. Carter's tailor shop, and Abbie could not move.

She stood rooted to the spot, shaking uncontrollably, her scarf still wrapped tightly around her face. The city felt so overwhelming; there were carts rushing by, and people jostling her, and so much noise and bustle everywhere she looked. But that was not what was truly frightening her.

If she turned around now, or froze time in this instant, then she would still be able to cling to hope; the hope that Robah Carter might be around that corner, waiting for her. But if she walked on and looked into that shop and he wasn't there... She would have to give up. And she didn't know if her heart could take it.

Patrick tugged at her hand as though she were a wayward mule. "Come on, Abbie," he said. "We're nearly there. I know you're tired."

"It's not that," said Abbie. She looked up at Patrick, trembling. "I'm so scared."

"What are you scared of?" asked her brother gently.

Abbie bit her lip. "I just... I'm scared that it's not him," she admitted. "And there's something else. Something much worse. I keep thinking of the way Papa looked... so broken. After Hawkins beat him. What if I drag Robah into that life, too? What if something happens to him because of me?"

Patrick put an arm around her shoulders. "Robah wanted you to tell him about Hawkins, didn't he?"

Abbie nodded.

"And still he wanted you after you told him, after he knew what danger he was in," said Patrick. "Abbie, sometimes we will hurt the people we love. Not because we want to, but just because we're human. Even if you didn't have the Hawkins problem, you would still be human – you would still have bad days and snappy moments and say things you don't mean. Danger is part of loving. But sometimes, it's the part that brings out the very best in us."

Abbie took a deep breath.

"Let's go," said Patrick softly.

She nodded, and then somehow her feet were carrying her forward, and they were walking into the cul-de-sac and all the shops were still broken down and empty except for the building where the tailor had been. There were new glass windows in it, and clothes displayed in them, and bright brass letters painted on the door.

R. Carter. Tailor.

Abbie felt her heart would burst. Surely, he wouldn't have come back here, to this very same shop where he'd worked before... surely this was nothing but a cruel coincidence. Yet her feet led her on, and Patrick was beside her, supporting her. The first snow had just begun to fall. It settled in great, perfect, white flakes on everything, and made her feel like she was on the inside of a fairy tale. She wasn't yet sure what kind.

She reached the front door and pushed it open slowly, half expecting an angry tailor to appear out of nowhere and scream at her. Instead, there was nothing. No one. The shop was empty. A few clothes on display, but no one behind the desk.

"He's not here," Abbie whispered.

Before Patrick could speak, another voice came from the back room. It was a glorious sound, this voice; it was like a ray of sunlight piercing through the clouds, shining on her face, warming everything.

"One moment."

Robah!

Abbie's knees nearly buckled. She leaned against Patrick, wanting to cry and scream and laugh and sing and dance all at once.

The back door of the shop opened, and he walked inside, looking strong and beautiful and more wonderful than even Abbie's fond imagination had remembered. He was wearing a well-cut navy suit that made him look taller somehow; he had grown a moustache, and it was neatly trimmed, his hair combed to one side. He looked perfect. He looked better than she had ever dreamed, and when his eyes rested on her, for a moment she feared that he wouldn't know this ragged little hermit girl with her wild hair and frightened eyes.

But he knew her. He knew her, and when she looked into his eyes, he saw that he loved her instantly.

"Abbie," he gasped, and held out his arms.

Abbie ran into them, and for a long moment, her whole world was nothing but the feeling of having his arms around her, the perfect way her body slotted against his, the steady thump of his heart against her ear. She felt she might have burst from sheer joy in that moment.

She stepped back, looking up at him. "Oh, Robah," she breathed.

"Abbie," he said again, and then bent and kissed her, and she drowned gloriously in that kiss; it felt like sinking into warm honey, utterly smooth and sweet.

It was another long moment before they came up for air, and Robah was stroking her face, her hair, her hands, and she couldn't take her eyes away from his. Patrick had discreetly withdrawn.

"It's you," she said. "It's really you."

"I thought…" Robah hesitated. "Oh, Abbie, you don't know how I've searched for you. When you never came back…"

Abbie's eyes filled with tears. "I'm so sorry."

"Don't cry. Please, my precious, precious Abbie, don't cry." Robah wiped her tears away with his thumb. "I thought something had happened. I thought Hawkins had found you. I've been searching for you all this time, every hour I had away from work, but in my heart, I thought you were gone."

A terrible shudder ran through Abbie. She looked over her shoulder, grabbing at her scarf again.

Robah put a hand over hers, looking puzzled. "Why are you doing that?" he said.

"He… he might find me," Abbie stammered fearfully.

Robah stared at her. "Oh, Abbie, don't you know?" he said, then looked away, tears filling his eyes. "Of course, you don't. How could you? You… you can't read the papers."

"Know what?" said Abbie breathlessly.

"I... well... right after you disappeared, the tailor closed up his shop, and I had no choice but to leave... I was an assistant for another tailor for a time, and while I was there, I met him." Robah's face hardened. "Hawkins. He came in for measurements. I took them, and of course, he thought me nothing but a dumb servant, so he was speaking with his friends all the time. They were planning to do something terrible to a girl who lived nearby. I followed them, and when they grabbed her, I called for the police. The police came in time to catch him almost in the act."

Robah cupped Abbie's face in her hands. "Don't you see, my darling? He's gone away. Of course, he won the court case, his father being the magistrate, but it was an awful scandal. It ruined the family. They were thrown into poverty, and Hawkins took his own life."

Abbie stared at him. "Hawkins is... is *dead*?" she said, her mind trying to grasp what Robah was telling her.

"For eight months now," said Robah. "That's how I was able to start the shop. The girl's fiancé gave me a reward... for helping her."

"Oh, Robah." Abbie flung her arms around his neck and buried her face in his chest. She burst into tears. "Is it true? Truly? Is it true?"

Robah's eyes were full of tears, too. He caressed her face gently. "It's true my love."

She stared at him, shaking her head. "Then I'm free?"

"Yes, my love. You are free."

"Truly and really free. I'm finally free." She started to laugh then, at first a choking sound as the truth settled into her. Leroy Hawkins gone? Leroy Hawkins never able to hurt her again. She squeezed her eyes shut and then opened them again. "I'm free…" she uttered again.

"Yes, you are." Robah's arms tightened around her, and he laughed with her, a deep and rumbling sound that shook her body. "All this time he's been gone…"

"You … you saved me." Abbie looked up at him. "Oh, Robah."

Robah grinned, his eyes sparkling, and seized her hand. "Come on," he said.

He pulled her to the door and pushed it open and pulled her out into the street. The snow was falling hard and fast now, and it made everything look magical, settling thickly on Robah's eyelashes. He spun her around and caught her against him, laughing. "You're free, Abbie." he said.

She couldn't take her eyes off him. "Yes," she whispered. "I'm free."

Then she reached up, tore off the scarf, and cast it to the winds.

And then she glanced around for Patrick. She couldn't wait to introduce him to Robah.

CHAPTER 19

❦

"Robah, hurry up," Abbie called, straightening up as she lifted a fresh rabbit pie out of the cast-iron stove. Its glorious scent filled the little galley kitchen, and she carried it into the dining room, setting it down on the polished oak table. Five places were set around it, and Abbie smiled down at it, her heart swelling with pride. There was nothing remotely extravagant about the meal, but she had folded the napkins and laid out the modest silverware with pride, and the plates were even made from china.

Now the only things that were still missing were their guests – who would arrive any minute – and her husband. Abbie tossed the dishcloth over her shoulder and walked down the hall toward their room. "Robah," she called. "They'll be here any minute."

She pushed the door open, and Robah was standing by the big window that she loved so much. It was open, and the warm summer air filled the room, touched with the faint scent of the marigolds that she had planted in the window-box she'd always wanted. Robah rested his arms on the sill, his white shirt stirring a little in the warm breeze.

Abbie came up behind him and wrapped her arms around him, resting her chin on his shoulder. He tipped his head back, snuggling into her.

"Are you all ready, Mrs. Carter?" he asked.

She giggled. Her new name still felt a little strange, even though it had been a month since they married. "I'm all ready, Mr. Carter," she said.

"Here they come." Robah nodded, and Abbie saw them approaching at the end of the street. Patrick was leading the way, his beard shaven now, but his moustache still gloriously red in the sunlight; he swung his arms freely, his broad chest thrust out. Gail followed beside him, wearing a pretty dress of her own making, all reds and yellows. Papa was on Patrick's arm, his walking stick digging energetically into the street.

"You know," said Robah, turning to Abbie and taking her into his arms, "you would have been enough. All my life, all I ever wanted was you, a perfect wife, and a tailor's shop of my own, and a little flat above it to keep my wife." He punctuated his words with kisses all over her face, making her giggle. "But I have gained even more than that. I've gained the family I never had."

Abbie gazed up at him adoringly. "And that family is free now, all thanks to you," she said. "You're my hero."

Robah leaned down and gave her a lingering kiss that sent shivers all the way down her spine. "You're my reason," he whispered, his eyes intensifying.

There was a knock at the door downstairs. Abbie giggled, kissing the end of his nose. "Shall we?" she said.

"We shall, my beautiful wife," said Robah.

He offered her his arm, and Abbie took it. Then they walked downstairs together, to open the door for their family.

The End

CONTINUE READING...

THANK you for reading **The Fishmongers Daughter!** **Are you wondering what to read next?** Why not read **The Shamed Little Matchgirl?** **Here's a sneak peek for you:**

Dinah Shaw hurried up the rickety stairs of the tenement building, her heart pounding with excitement despite the icy drafts that found their way through the holes in the thin, shaky walls. Her right hand was firmly clutched around the small, skinny arm of her five-year-old brother; in her left, she carried something she considered to be a great treasure. It crinkled and rustled promisingly in her hand. Despite the hunger gnawing at the pit of her stomach, Dinah gave a little giggle of happy anticipation.

"Slow down, Di," complained her brother's little voice by her side. "I can't keep up."

"Oh, sorry, Ollie." Dinah slowed a little, tugging at Ollie to bring him beside her. "I just can't believe that I've found a whole entire newspaper. And it's not even wet. It's perfect."

"Mama will take it if she sees you with it," said Ollie.

Dinah looked down into his wide, worried eyes. They were softest brown and looked enormous in his pinched face. "It's a good thing Mama isn't here then," she said, trying to keep her tone as light as she could. "By the time she gets back, I'll be done with it. We'll stuff it into that gap in the wall and she won't even notice."

Ollie's face brightened. "The gap right above your side of the pallet?"

"That's right," said Dinah, wincing at the memory of every cold night spent under that howling draft.

"Oh, good," said Ollie. "Let's go put it in the gap right away."

"Not yet," laughed Dinah. "Newspapers are for reading, Ollie."

"Mama says there's no reason to learn to read," said Ollie. "She says you're a fool for trying it, and that it's no use."

Dinah felt a familiar hurt blaze across her heart. She was fairly certain that Mama hated reading simply because she had never learned herself, and for some reason that Dinah would never understand, the written word frightened her. But she couldn't say that to Ollie. She forced a smile instead. "Maybe I am a bit silly, then," she said, "but we've got to do something to keep busy while Mama's out, don't we? Besides, you can play with the boys while I'm busy."

"Yes." Ollie's face brightened. "Bobby found some nails in the street last week. We're using them as soldiers."

Click Here to Continue Reading!
https://www.ticahousepublishing.com/victorian-romance.html

THANKS FOR READING

IF YOU LOVE VICTORIAN ROMANCE, **Click Here**

https://victorian.subscribemenow.com/

to hear about all **New Faye Godwin Romance Releases! I will let you know as soon as they become available!**

Thank you, Friends! If you enjoyed ***The Fishmonger's Daughter,*** would you kindly take a couple minutes to leave a positive review on Amazon? It only takes a moment, and positive reviews truly make a difference. Thank you so much! I appreciate it!

Much love,

Faye Godwin

MORE FAYE GODWIN VICTORIAN ROMANCES!

We love rich, dramatic Victorian Romances and have a library of Faye Godwin titles just for you! (Remember that ALL of Faye's Victorian titles can be downloaded FREE with Kindle Unlimited!)

CLICK HERE to discover Faye's Complete Collection of Victorian Romance!

https://ticahousepublishing.com/victorian-romance.html

ABOUT THE AUTHOR

Faye Godwin has been fascinated with Victorian Romance since she was a teen. After reading every Victorian Romance in her public library, she decided to start writing them herself —which she's been doing ever since. Faye lives with her husband and young son in England. She loves to travel throughout her country, dreaming up new plots for her romances. She's delighted to join the Tica House Publishing family and looks forward to getting to know her readers.

contact@ticahousepublishing.com